A
Woman's Secret

C.L. Koch

ISBN 978-1-936556-35-9

Published 2018

Published by Black Velvet Seductions Publishing

A Woman's Secret Copyright 2018 C.L. Koch
Cover design Copyright 2018 Jessica Greeley

Dedicated to my mother Toni Frey with love and gratitude.
The strongest woman I have known.

Acknowledgements

I would like to thank my husband, Bill, and daughter, Misty, for their love, support and belief in me, Heide Nash, Alice White, author, Velda Brotherton, author, and all the members of the Arkansas Ridge Writers Critique group, as well as everyone at Black Velvet Seductions for their hard work in making this book shine brightly.

Chapter One

Dawn broke over the fog covered hills above the manor house in central England. Fingers of sunlight tickled their way through the tree branches and pushed through the windowpanes onto the sleeping face of young Hannah. She pushed the covers away, pulled a cloak over her shoulders, and stood before the single window of her bedroom and gazed up at the horned moon.

"Mother, why did you die so sudden?" A chill ran down her spine. She pulled the cloak a litter tighter.

A knock on the door turned her away from the window.

"Enter."

The door opened, a maid stepped into the room with a curtsy.

"Yes Sarah?"

"Your father is on his way up. He asked me to wake you. Since you are already awake, would you like me anything before he arrives?"

Hannah's eyes darted to the wedding dress hanging in the corner of the room. "Bring my breakfast up and after he leaves you may begin dressing me."

"Yes ma'am." Sarah bobbed her head and slipped through the doorway closing the door behind her.

Turning back to the window, she smiled gazing out across to the little family church. "Today I become Lady Hannah."

The sound of heavy boots on the stairs rang out as a warning her father was on his way up to her. She opened the door and took a seat beside her writing table. The thought of leaving him alone in this big manor house hurt her heart. Perhaps this was best for him, having her safe, married and in France; he could get on with his life. A handsome man of his age could remarry.

"Good morrow my daughter. I would like a few moments with you before the wedding." Edward paused inside the doorway.

Hannah stood and bowed her head. "Yes Father, of course. Would you like to have a seat?"

"No. I should like to stand for this. This should not take long."

"As you wish Father."

His tone gave her cause to for concern, as she remained standing in front of him. Once again, a chill ran down her spine.

This could not be good news.

Chapter Two

Sarah hesitated outside the door, balancing, on one hand, a silver serving tray that held her mistress's breakfast, not knowing whether to let her presence known. Concentrating on holding the tray steady, she did not make a sound. Her head tilted against the sturdy English oak door, listening to the voices on the other side. Lord Bingham's deep tones carried through the door with ease, but she was having difficulty hearing Mistress Hannah's soft voice.

"Yes, I signed the marriage contract months ago. And yes, I know this is what you think you want. However, I have my doubts. You are my only child," Edward said. "Perhaps you could go to court and be one of Queen Elizabeth's ladies in waiting?"

"Father, I have never wished to go to court. Life there only brings unhappiness. This is my wedding day. I love Thomas, and want nothing more than to be his wife." Hannah's voice was adamant. "You have known his family for years. You continue to have business dealings with his father even though he now resides in France. I do not understand this sudden change in your opinion of him."

"It is because of business, I am having doubts. England, the throne, business, everything is unstable. If the Privy Council should arrange a marriage with Spain for Queen Elizabeth, England could be at war with France, or the other way around. I will not have you in harm's way."

Sarah could hear heavy footfalls on the floor, Lord Bingham only paced when he was troubled. All of the house staff knew to tread light and become invisible when he walked the floor.

"Thomas will keep me safe. Father, you must not doubt his devotion to me." Hannah spoke softly.

"His devotion is not in question. Any young man would want to wed a beautiful young woman who is heir to a manor and estates. William

Cecil is in the process of expanding his web of informants to protect the throne. Through those he has already placed, I can neither discover where Thomas goes nor what he does when he is not involved in his father's business."

"You had him followed? You spied on him? You think he has chosen me to wife for money and estates?"

Sobs drifted through the door.

"Yes, Hannah I did have his activities observed. Any man interested in my only child and heir would be treated the same. Thomas is not the man I would have chosen for you, but having you in France is the only way I can see to secure your future. His father and I were friends long before his self—imposed exile to France when Mary took the throne. I know and respect the father. I do not know the son well. His movements are kept secret while he goes about his father's business." Edward's voice softened. "You also know the difficulty I have saying *no* to you. I have never denied you anything you've had your heart set on, especially after your mother died, and I may be guilty of trying to make up for her death by spoiling you. This is why I had to ask you, before this goes any further, if you are certain you wish to wed today."

"Yes, father. I love Thomas. Above all else, I wish to be his wife. I know we will have the same successful marriage you and mother had. Father please; allow Thomas a chance to prove to you what a good man he is. In time you will learn to love him as the son you never had."

"As you wish, my dearest. I shall not ask you again. However, I have news from France. Thomas's father has taken a turn for the worst. He has requested his son's immediate return. I have arranged for you, Thomas, and both of your servants on board one of my carracks due to set sail on the morrow. The ship is more for cargo than for passengers. I am sure the captain shall do his best to make room for the four of you. I leave you now and go inform Thomas. You may inform Sarah of this change in departure. I do not know how she will react taking leave of her mother sooner than intended."

There was a pause. Sarah took this cue to tap on the door.

"Come." Hannah's voice carried through the door.

Sarah entered the room deft hands balanced the tray. With her head down, she hurried across the room to place her mistress's breakfast on the oak writing table beside the native rock fireplace. When she turned, Edward kissed Hannah on the forehead before he left the room.

Hannah stood in front of the window, looking out. "It is a good morrow, milady, and a bright beautiful morning for a wedding."

"Most certainly, Sarah," Hannah replied.

"I have brought your breakfast, milady. I cannot let you face your wedding day on an empty stomach."

Hannah's fingers traced the diamond—shaped, leaded, windowpanes as she turned to Sarah. "Where is everyone?"

Sarah smiled and pulled out a straight—backed chair for Hannah to sit at the table to eat. "Mother is in the garden directing the younger maids on cutting the flowers for the church and the wedding feast tables." Sarah made her way to the large oak trunk in the corner of the room containing Hannah's wedding clothes. "The kitchen is a beehive of activity with the cook herself queen bee. She is shouting at everyone, then praising them. However, I suppose you are more interested in the whereabouts of your young man." Sarah flashed a wicked smile. "He is barricaded in his room, being tended to by his horrible French servant. Phillip would not even allow the maid to take in breakfast. Said he alone would ready his lord today. Oh so silly if you ask me, a grown man acting as though he were attending to the King of France himself. Thank goodness Englishmen are not so pretentious."

"You have never been to court." Hannah giggled while she watched Sarah lay out her kirtle, bodice, and petticoat, on the bed, arranging them with the undergarments on top, and held up the deep blue wedding dress.

Hannah sprang to her feet, poured water from the pitcher and washed her hands and face. Once completing the task, she moved to the center of her room and allowed Sarah to dress her with each layer of clothing. The wedding dress was of the finest blue linen and white lace with matching silk shoes and netherstocks.

"Oh dear." Sarah stepped back and looked Hannah over from head to toe. Tears filled her eyes.

"What is wrong? Do I look hideous?" She looked down at the dress and turned around.

"No, milady. I was taken by surprise. You look so much like the portrait of your mother, Mistress Victoria, God rest her soul, the one hanging in your father's study." Sarah blinked, sniffled, and made the sign of the cross. "You have the look of her, except your hair is a darker brown, like your father's." Smiling, she placed her hands on her thin hips; her own young frame was covered in a modest white linen smock, under a matching dark green wool skirt with matching woolen bodice, which tugged her bodice into place. "Please sit down milady, so I can tie your slippers."

Hannah relaxed, taking a seat on a stool. "Sarah, we are alone. Stop with the formalities, I cannot abide it today. Father has received word from France. Thomas is to return at once. This means we shall be leaving shortly after the wedding feast."

Kneeling, Sarah nodded her head and tied the slippers into place, glanced up and quickly looked away. "There, they match perfectly. Now we must put your hair up."

"Sarah, did you hear what I said?"

"Yes, we shall leave this day for France."

"You have nothing further to say on the matter?"

"My mother has served your family since the day she married my father. She continued to serve after his death. I was ten years old when I began to assist your mother after you were born and have been your maid ever since. I am glad we are departing today. I have no wish to live my entire life here, ending up wed to some man of your father's choosing. Living a life as my mother has, never knowing what the rest of the world is like. I want more in my life. My mother knows this. She does not agree with me but she accepts what is in my nature to do."

"I wish for your courage. I have doubts of what our lives hold for us."

"Milady, please. All will be well for you."

Hannah whispered. "Check the hallway, we must speak."

Frowning, Sarah went to the door. She peered both ways, closed the door and eased the latch into place.

Hannah moved to the bed and patted the coverlet indicating Sarah should sit. Sarah did so with her hands folded in her lap.

In hushed tones, Hannah spoke. "I must do my duty as a wife. I can run a household, manage the expenses and the like. But there are other wifely duties I must also carry out. I have heard the maids talking about the intimacies transpiring between a man and a woman. They speak of private duties, lewd wanton ways, and consummating the marriage." Hannah blushed.

"They giggle and tell tales of amorous attentions and trysts in the fields. They prattle on about barn animals. Do not listen to them." Sarah's tone was serious.

"I am afraid. Sarah, I am so afraid. I have also overheard conversations about how some women do not enjoy intimacy, while others are wanton. I hope Thomas will be gentle and patient with me." She paused.

"But what if I disappoint him? What if I am wanton and he turns away from me? What if I am not to his liking?" She blushed seeing the look of shock on Sarah's face. "There, I said it aloud." Hannah exhaled.

"I see." Sarah reached out and took her hand. "It is expected for you to be experiencing these emotions. Be assured, all brides ask these same questions. They have done so in the past and will continue to do so in the future. Your mother's premature death has left your education wanting."

"I think what I truly need to know is what to do? I have no one else to ask." She squeezed Sarah's hand.

It was Sarah's turn to take a deep breath. "Intimacy is a natural act between man and woman. Women come to the marriage bed virginal. The same is not true for the groom."

She jerked her hand back. "Have care, Sarah. Are you trying to tell me Thomas has been unfaithful to me?"

"No, no, of course not. I am only saying, experience with such matters is a man's duty. Men are expected to have had their frolicking fun with other women before taking a wife. Some continue to do so by taking a mistress. You remember the stories about King Henry. Does anyone truly know how many women graced his bed over the course of his life?" Sarah smiled. "Think about it. Can you picture a member of the court standing outside the king's bedchamber? Parchment and quill in hand, making little tally marks when women departed after the deed was done."

Hannah laughed. "Thank you. I needed something to lighten the moment. You are right. He will have had experience in this area and I have nothing to fear." Hannah leaned over and hugged Sarah. "Tonight it will all be over."

"This is not an arranged marriage. You love him! He loves you. He will cherish you as his wife. All will be well." Sarah took her by the hands and pulled her to her feet. Hannah took a seat on the stool and their conversation turned to the design of hair.

The loud knock drew Hannah's attention. She turned to Sarah and nodded in the direction of the door. Sarah opened it, bowed to Lord Bingham and then she slipped in silence out into the hallway closing the door.

Edward stood with his hands behind his back; he was dressed in black, his custom since the death of her mother. More than a year had passed since she died. He should have put away his mourning clothes.

Hannah put on her brightest smile. *Still he cannot bring himself to end his mourning. Not even for my wedding. Constant in his grief, the years have been kind to his face. He has only a few wrinkles about the corners of his eyes when he smiles.* She watched his eyes take in every inch of her.

He smiled. "I had no idea you were planning to wear your mother's dress. You are beautiful my dear." He took a deep breath. "There is a scent of lavender. Victoria loved lavender."

"I found dried sprigs in the trunk when Sarah and I were making ready for today." Her long thin fingers trembled under her father's gaze. He wavered. She clutched his arm. "Father, are you well? Do you need to sit?"

"No, no, I'm fine." He patted her hand to reassure her. "It is just — I saw you standing there, and for a moment, the room began to spin and my vision narrowed, taking me back in time to another beautiful woman standing before me wearing same dress with the smell of lavender about her. She smiled the exact same smile. Her green eyes looking up at me. For a moment, I thought you were your mother. You look so much like her. You are as beautiful as she was in this dress."

"Except my hair is darker than mother's." Relieved her father was not ill, she could not help but regret her mother was not here today.

Edward put his arms around her and embraced her. She returned his hug, and could feel the warmth and love pour from him. He took a step back and presented a small dark leather box. "I believe this will add the finishing touch." He handed it to her with a smile.

She raised the lid. Her heart leapt when she recognized the five green teardrop emeralds dangling from a silver chain laying on a bed of black velvet.

"Oh! Father, it is beautiful! I remember the last time mother wore this. It was our dressmaking trip to London two years ago. You introduced us to Thomas."

"These are the emeralds I gave your mother on our wedding night. They are yours now. I know she would have given them to you and would be honored for you to wear them today." He took the necklace out of the box, stepped behind her and fastened it around her neck.

Hannah crossed the room to stand before the mirror of polished silver. Her mother's face looked back at her. Her own dark hair hung in curls from the crown of her head where tiny white wild flowers were set in contrast. Tears overcame her eyes and spilled down her cheeks. She turned to her father, whose eyes had also pooled with tears. "Thank you Father, I am the one who is honored to wear them."

Edward stepped forward and placed his weathered hands on her small shoulders. She looked up at him. A hint of concern the only blot in his firm shaven face.

His black doublet was spotless and fitted his still muscular frame well. He looked down at her, standing straight and tall, every inch of him imposing.

His face softened and kissed his daughter's forehead. Then, stepping to her side, he held out his hand for hers.

"All are awaiting the bride, if you are ready?"

Placing her hand on his she looked about the bedchamber.

Oh mother, how I wish you were here this day.

"Yes father, I am ready."

Chapter Three

Edwards's private parlor was small, intimate and sparsely furnished. The flames in the fireplace crackled filling the room with much—needed warmth and the scent of peat smoke. His greatest vanity books and ledgers filled the shelves lining the opposite wall. He hoped had instilled his love of books in his only child, over the years they had spent in this room. Now she is the wife of a man he could not trust nor shake off the feeling of ill ease at the thought of his son—in—law.

A sideboard held a pitcher of ale and two pewter pints. William filled the pints, listening to Edward. "The throne is still unstable. Queen Elizabeth must marry and God only knows whom. Parliament, the Privy Council, and the Pope will all have their say. There are too many variables." Shaking his head, Edward paused. "I have word from Cecil of Walsingham's quiet return to England. His journey is not public. I will meet with him before he returns to France. You and I shall continue as planned until I know more." Edward stood before the table, hands behind his back.

"Pirates have become quite bothersome in open water. Some are well organized, most are not. Word on the docks is no ship is safe." William smiled, sitting the pints on the end of the table. He traced the Irish shore with his finger on the worn leather map lying before them. His broad shoulders hunched over the table, a thong of leather held his long, dark auburn hair back at the nape of his neck. "They must have a safe port somewhere along here. The quay is here." He pointed to a spot on the map. "Going to ruin, although a small supply ship can still dock. I think we can have the inlet and quay operational in a short time."

"I agree on the safe port." Edward leaned over for a closer look. "I am prepared to move forward with our plans to repair the quay. Our primary reason to keep the land well—armed and protected is to provide a safe haven in Ireland for your ships, as well as mine. Men will have to be trained at arms and well paid to remain loyal." Edward studied the point on the map. Staying focused on the task was difficult. He still worried about Hannah. "There is no one I trust more than you to see this done. I have a shipment of supplies under way. We should keep the renovations as quiet as possible."

"All of my business in England is done for now," William said. "I will be able to give the repairs and security my full attention. Rebuilding the quay should not pose a problem; the harbor is hidden deep inside the bay. With defense in mind, a strategically placed guard can alert us to any unwelcome ship. Another advantage is the shallows are difficult to navigate if the pilot is unfamiliar with the waters."

"Well done." Edward turned away to face the window. "I have ordered supplies, tools, and such. The ship should arrive there in a fortnight." His body tensed and his mind would not stay focused. The wedding had been a mistake. How could he end the marriage without breaking his daughter's heart?

William broke the silence. "Still something troubles you."

"Ah, yes. Hannah has made her choice. Since her mother's death I fear I have not been good with saying no to her." Edward paced. "Something does not quite ring true with my new son—in—law. I have had no direct contact from his father since Thomas arrived here. This is so unlike Robert. Not one reply to any of my correspondences. Not one! Now this sudden need to return to France immediately after the nuptials."

"If my memory serves me, you and Robert met at court."

"Correct, we became quite close in those days. We have been involved in many endeavors since. The year his wife was with child, Robert lived here. In the months that followed Queen Mary taking the throne, he moved his family to France. I have his letter here," he indicated a wooden chest resting on the mantle, "stating his plans to return to England after Elizabeth's coronation. I also have the last message I received from him, informing me of his son temporarily acting in his stead due to illness, over two years ago. Nor did I hear from him when Victoria died. He sent nothing during the marriage contract negotiations. Not one word." His pace quickened.

"Calm yourself, Edward." He lifted a pint across the table and continued, "Here, drink. Are you certain the signature on the contract is Robert's?"

"Yes. Yes, of course. I know his heavy scrawl as well as I know Hannah's delicate script." Accepting the pint, he took a long draught and shook his head. "Perhaps I am a jealous father who does not want another man taking my daughter away."

"I believe there may be more to this. I have never seen you so distraught."

"A simple, uncomplicated marriage is what I wished for Hannah. This is a new beginning for her. I allowed her to have a say in the choice, but I swear something is most wrong."

"I cannot pretend to be detached from your worries. What would you have me do?"

"Depart on the same ship carrying Hannah to France. And take with you the names of my contacts there." Edward handed a leather pouch to William. He could think of no other way to proceed. "Gather any information they may have on Robert. Then, I would have you see him in person."

"I will. Anything else?" He tucked the folded leather into his doublet.

"Yes. See my daughter safely to France and her new home." Relief flooded him. Still, he had another plan formulating. He would send another missive to Robert by way of Thomas, another test.

"I shall endeavor to uncover all possible information to ease your mind."

"Store up your knowledge for the throne of England as well, my friend. In addition, I do not wish for Hannah to know the reasons you are going to France. She need not know more of my doubts concerning her husband. Unlike his father, Thomas is too reckless." Edward was calm for the first time today. William had never failed him in the past. He would not fail him where Hannah was concerned.

William placed his empty tankard on the table. "If I depart now, I can be aboard before the bride and groom arrive. I understand the captain was able to make the accommodations you requested?"

"Yes. With the right amount of coin, anything is possible. He has given up his own small cabin for the two women." Edward raised his tankard and smiled.

"Will that be all?"

"Yes. Except, remember to keep an eye on the new broadsheets, seems remarkable no one has puzzled out our ruse." Edward chuckled. "The dregs of wit, indeed."

"A ruse to blind the people of the true weight of these difficult times." William smiled and left the room.

Edward downed the last of his pint and paced once again. His mind returned to the wedding, he stopped in front of the portrait of his wife.

"Victoria, I wish you were here to tell me I have done right by our daughter, and for England," he said to the beloved face smiling down on him. Turning away, he rolled up the map and replaced it on the bookshelf. He walked to the window and saw his daughter and her husband talking to their guests. Hannah has the look of her mother, no doubt. She stood with the sun reflecting off the gold band on her finger. "I know she misses you also," he whispered, looking up at the portrait. Tears filled his eyes. "Our home will never be the same with both of you gone."

Chapter Four

The courtyard abandoned of guests, except for a couple of cats snatching savory morsels of meat from the unattended tables. Thomas watched Phillip make his way through the maids and boys who cleaned up after the wedding feast. He would have preferred to skip all the celebrating. Their last conversation had been about returning to France and to the life to which they were both accustomed.

Thomas watched Phillip wind his way through the melee. He carried two pints held at arm's length as if he were afraid the contents of the vessels might splash onto his expensive clothes. For as long as he had known the Frenchman, Phillip always had the best and most expensive of everything, from the cut of his hair down to the fine leather boots on his feet. Thomas smiled as his friend approached.

"Where is your fresh young bride?" Phillip smirked and offered him one of the flagons.

"Having a tearful farewell scene with dear old father, I suspect." Thomas took the glass of ale and downed it in one gulp, and nodded his head in the direction of Hannah and her father deep in conversation with a portly woman across the garden.

"Ah, the dutiful child has now become the dutiful wife. You have enchanted her where all others have failed. She is wedded and soon to be bedded." He sneered.

"Phillip, you are drunk," Thomas snarled. This was not something he wished to discuss.

Phillip held his arms wide and bowed. "Not nearly so drunk as I should be. These English do not know what good wine is." He frowned and gazed into the tankard, and shrugged a shoulder.

"Why you must drink is beyond me. I pay you huge amounts of money every month. You spend the majority on women and drink as if it were nothing. Women throw themselves at you, only to be disgusted by your perverse appetites and then you play the broken—hearted fool. You know what is at stake here. If you are not up to this, then I will find someone else." Thomas looked down his thin nose.

"My Lord, your words wound me. I ask your pardon for having displeased you. I have made the arrangements you asked for. All is ready, I swear. We shall depart shortly and sail on the morrow, docking in Le Havre in two days if the winds are with us. The ship will stop in Cherbourg to offload cargo late tomorrow. We will have to spend only two nights on board the ship." Phillip took a drink, grimaced, and continued. "Once we arrive in France, we shall make short our travel over land and you will be home with your dutiful wife beside you."

"You have done well, Phillip. I just want this to be over." He waved his free hand. "My plan is going just like we discussed. We have worked too hard to fail now. England sits on the very precipice of ruin. This, bastard child of a whore, Elizabeth cannot remain on the throne. The northern earls will not follow her. We must be in place before her downfall. Nothing can go wrong."

"Nothing will go wrong, I assure you, my Lord. You have my undying loyalty. I will see this through to the end." Phillip glanced around. "Here comes your new father—in—law. This is where I take my leave, my Lord." He bowed again and walked away.

"Thomas! May I have a word with you?" Edward approached.

"Of course, what can I do for you Sir?" Thomas moved his hands behind his back and straightened his shoulders.

What could this old fool possibly have to say?

"Hannah is seeing the last of the family off. This is most likely the only opportunity I will have to speak to you privately."

Edward's words caught him off guard. Thomas held his breath and smiled. "This must be most serious, Sir." He had a nagging presage this was not going to be good.

"No, just business." He handed a leather pouch to Thomas. "I would have you deliver a business proposition to your father."

Thomas took the packet. "I will gladly make the delivery."

"There is one other matter I would like to discuss with you." His face became hard. "I love my daughter above all else. You were not my first choice in a husband for her."

Thomas opened his mouth to reply, but Edward held up a hand to silence him. "Now it is time for me to tell you something Hannah will never know. Do you understand?"

"Yes, Sir." He did not like this turn in the conversation.

"You will continue to make her happy. If you break her heart, or harm her in any way, you will discover there is nowhere you can hide. I will hunt you down, I will find you, and I will kill you. Do you understand?" The older man glared at him.

"Yes Sir. I assure you, she will be well taken care of." He contained the rage exploding inside. How dare this whoreson make threats?

"Have care." Edward turned and walked away.

"As you will be taken care of." Smiling, Thomas watched him go and turned toward the stable. The only thing left was to see the carriage was ready to take them to the dock. The sight of England fading on the horizon was all he wanted now.

The dowry, packed away in a small trunk that would accompany them, was a goodly sum. Enough to pay his expenses over the coming few years—expenses his father need not be concerned with, for Thomas had plans to raise his family to the right hand of the legitimate English crown. Only one more thing to take care of. Perhaps an accident would tidy things up. Should it be at sea or on land? He smiled as he walked. Either way, it was a minor detail. He was good with details.

Chapter Five

The carriage ride to the dock was, for the most part, uneventful. Hannah had said farewell to all of the servants, tenants and their families, leaving her father for last. They had parted with her promise to return for Christmas. She waved farewell until the four matching black geldings made the first bend in the road and she lost sight of everyone. The dray bounced and lurched along the road.

Hannah gazed out the window as they jostled along the English countryside. Her thoughts were of the man sitting beside her. Thomas had been quiet with formal politeness to her since their marriage vows. He was attentive but aloof, she was nervous but never thought that he might be also. This long silence between the two of them was uncommon. She glanced to her left and regarded the blank expression on his face directed toward her. Was he thinking that their marriage had been a mistake? The thought caught her breath, and she worried the fabric of her skirt. Here was the man she loved. The man she wanted to spend the rest of her life with, have children and grow old with, and he was unusually quiet. Perhaps he was concerned about his father? Of the four in the carriage, she alone knew the pain of losing a parent.

The road wound around through trees hundreds of years old, whose branches created a canopy above the carriage. Fingers of sunlight pierced through the dense foliage. Birds sat quiet on tree branches and appeared cautious as the carriage passed them by. The scent of decaying leaves and wild flowers drifted through the window. Hannah breathed deeply and closed her eyes in an attempt to calm her nerves. Moments became hours. Hours passed. Hannah slept.

"Awake, Madam, we have arrived," Thomas announced.

Opening her eyes, she was surprised to find her head on his shoulder. She glanced through the window, "Indeed we have."

He helped her down from the carriage and he tensed when she took his hand. Perhaps tonight, their wedding night, alone with him, there would be the opportunity to ask him how his father was fared.

He led her the short distance to the gangway and on to the ship's deck and then steered her to the railing overlooking the dock. Phillip and Sarah followed close behind.

"Madam, if you would be so kind as to wait here, while Phillip and I take the maid below to make ready your room and secure our belongings before we sail."

"Of course, my husband," she answered with her sweetest smile. The last thing she wanted was to be alone. Her smile never faltered, being the obedient wife. Anxiety built up inside, and she squeezed the ship's railing with both hands, her knuckles turning white inside her gloves. She forced herself to take in the activity on the dock before her.

Torches sparked to life up and down on both sides of the dock, lighting the way for last minute cargo and supplies brought aboard. The smelled of dead, rotting fish and brine accosted her. She wrinkled her nose with disgust and forced her hands to relax their grip. Biting her lower lip, she heard a familiar voice behind her.

"Your husband has abandoned you so soon?"

"William!" she whirled around. "No, not at all, the—I mean he has gone below to make sure all is well." Her gaze swept the deck in hopes of seeing Thomas. "What are you doing here?"

"As it happens, your father has me headed to France on business. What a delightful happenstance, we shall be sailing together!" He smiled down at her, placing her hand in the bend of his elbow and leading her to the other side of the ship. "However, Thomas should never have left you alone. It is not safe for any female to be left unescorted in the company of deckhands."

"You sound like father," she smiled. "How did you get here before us?"

"I am employed by your father to look after all of his interests. As for my arrival, I left the manor by horse after the wedding feast. I have been on board for a couple of hours." He led her to a barrel, where a jug of ale sat beside a cloth covered wooden tray. He removed the fabric, revealing cheese and dark bread, poured the ale into a pewter mug and placed it in front of her.

"Are you telling me I have been reduced from beloved daughter to a mere interest?" she teased.

"You are the beat of your father's heart. Since your mother's death, you and you alone are his most valued interest. Never forget that, not even for a moment."

"William you have always taken good care of my father's business interests. I shall never doubt my father's love for me. And I shall never allow him to doubt my love for him." She took a drink of ale.

"You have grown into a most intelligent young lady. And, now I shall endeavor to continue your education. The captain says we shall sail on schedule at first light on the morrow. This being your first voyage at sea, there is a most unladylike malaise you should avoid, the dreaded sea sickness. The trick to not succumbing to sea sickness is to always have something in your stomach." He waved his hands and puffed up his chest to emphasize his mock drama.

She giggled while he broke off a chunk of firm, heavy, dark bread and handed it to her. She chewed it, realizing that she was indeed hungry and took in her surroundings. Men of all shapes and sizes scurried in different directions across the deck. Lanterns hung about the ship providing enough illumination to prevent the sailors from running into one another. The brightness of the lanterns reflected off the brass fittings throughout the railing of the ship, and scuffed and worn English oak of the deck floor. She continued to watch the bustle of activity until she felt William's eyes on her.

"This will truly work?" Indicating the food before her, she turned her attention back to him.

William produced a dirk to slice the cheese. "Yes, plus I know you have, most likely, not eaten since your wedding feast."

She smiled remembering this day she became a wife, and took a bite of the sharp, pungent cheese with some bread, washing the two down with the ale.

"I should have known that you would be here to steal *my* wife away the moment my back is turned!" Thomas stepped between them.

"You would do best to never turn your back to me, should you ever again leave her unattended." William slammed down the jug and stormed into the darkness of the ship.

Chapter Six

"Thomas I do not understand!" She looked up at him as they stood in front of the door.

"Hannah this is a cargo ship not the local inn. You and your handmaid have the captain's quarters. Phillip and I will find sleeping accommodations in the hold. You do not understand the danger Sarah would encounter if she were left alone. Phillip cannot look to her safety."

"I know very well what this is. God's teeth. I also know this is our wedding night and I expected to spend it with my husband." She raised her voice and her face grew hot with anger and embarrassment having said it aloud.

"I am vexed by your words as I am by your behavior. Curb your temper, you forget yourself madam." His eyes bore into hers.

"Yes, yes, you are correct. I was not thinking. Sarah and I will of course share this cabin." Hannah lowered her head in defeat.

Thomas leaned in and opened the door for her. She accepted his kiss upon her cheek. "Good even, madam." He closed the door behind her.

"Good even, my husband," she whispered leaning against the door and fought back tears. Sudden movement in the dim light startled her.

"Mistress, are you ill?" Sarah stepped forward with a candle in hand.

"I am fine, Sarah. I, I am weary. The day has been long and has made me weep. All will be set right on the morrow after a night's sleep."

"Yes, milady, I will light another candle and help you ready for bed."

"Thank you Sarah." Hannah looked around their small room and felt the motion of the ship for the first time. She grasped the small table attached to the wall to steady herself. Then, she felt a gentle swaying back and forth as if the ship was going to rock her to sleep. Sarah began unlacing her travel dress.

Taking in her surroundings, Hannah found the room was indeed small and the walls appeared to be dark grey. She noticed only a single bed in the room. This was not a bed made for two, but Sarah had made herself a pallet on the floor. A single chair, a stool and her travel trunk made up the rest of the room.

The smell of tallow candles along with a strong musty odor penetrated her nostrils. She wished she had some rosemary to cast on the floor. Her eyes returned to the narrow bed. A well—worn and dented chamber pot sat under one end of the narrow bed and she moved to sit on the chair, while the maid poured a pint of ale.

"Pour yourself one. This has been a long day for both of us." Hannah attempted to hold back a yawn and she took a long drink.

"Thank you, milady."

"God's teeth, Sarah, I will not have you calling me anything but my own name when we are alone. Twice today I have told you this."

"I suppose I thought things would be different now you are wed."

"What do you mean?" She was confused, her thoughts drifting back to Thomas.

"My mother said I would have to learn new ways since I would be living in a new country. Master Phillip said I would have to remember my place as a maid in Master Thomas's household. I—"

"No Sarah," Hannah suppressed a yawn. "Nothing will ever alter between the two of us when we are alone. No matter how change abounds around us. Nevertheless, it does seem that we both have much to learn. No matter what Thomas commands, it must be done." She handed her maid the empty pint. "Put the candle out and go to bed."

Hannah watched Sarah blow out the candle on the table leaving the lamp suspended from the ceiling lit. She pulled the covers tightly about herself. Her last thoughts were of her husband and her new home.

Awakened by a knock on the door, Hannah heard voices. After a cat like stretch, she opened her eyes to find the room was no bigger in the daylight.

Sarah spoke to someone and turned her back to the doorway. The motion of the ship forced her to set aside the cloth covered wooden tray before closing the door.

"Good morrow, milady. Would you like to eat?" She indicated the tray. "Or would you like to dress first?"

"I shall eat first. I would hate to soil my clothing and have to dress all over again."

Sarah moved the tray to the bed next to her and took a seat on the other side of the tray. Hannah ate commenting on the fresh baked bread and fish. She noticed her maid ate little, playing with her food. They took turns washing in the bucket attached to the wall. The water was salty and cold.

"Let's go for a walk on deck after we dress." Hannah was hopeful of finding Thomas.

"As you wish," Sarah replied with little enthusiasm in her voice.

The maid laid out Hannah's kirtle, bodice and petticoat, and helped her dress. She made a slight whimper and dash for the chamber pot, and proceeded to spew what little breakfast she had just eaten. Breaking into a sweat, pale as death, she gagged and dry heaved clinging to the side of the bed.

After she finished, Hannah steadied her. "Come, you are getting into the bed. Not the floor. And here you will stay." She picked up the coarse blankets from the pallet and added them to the ones on the bed.

A knock on the door drew her away from her patient. She opened it to find Thomas. He immediately took a step away from the smell of vomit wafting from the room. A look of disgust crossed his face; his hand was quick to cover his nose and mouth.

"Thomas, I am so glad to see you. Sarah is very ill. Could you find someone to empty the pot and bring more water?"

"I will send someone," he turned away, disappearing up the steps.

She propped the door open to allow some fresh air into the room. When Sarah was sick again, Hannah bathed her hands, and face with the brackish water and pushed her hair back out of her eyes and face. She pulled the chair beside the bed and sat. Before long, a small boy appeared in the doorway with a bucket of fresh water and he replaced the offensive pot with a clean one.

Sarah lay on the bed moaning and holding her stomach. She gagged and heaved but nothing else filled the pot. Hannah pulled a book from her trunk and sat beside her motionless maid. She had read a couple of chapters aloud when Phillip appeared in the doorway holding a tray.

"A bit of broth for Miss Sarah. The cook says it will help her to sleep. And...if she is sleeping, she will not be...you know...doing the other."

"That is most kind of you Phillip. Thank you."

"I am fond of Miss Sarah and wanted to help her," he stammered looking embarrassed. "I must go. Thomas is waiting for me. A game of Primero is starting up on deck."

"Of course, thank you again." She smiled at him taking the tray.

Hannah helped Sarah into a seated position placing the bowl of broth in her hands. "That was a whole new side of Phillip I have never seen before." Hannah shook her head in puzzlement. "I wonder what has come over him."

Sarah sipped the warm, bitter, liquid. "At least the broth seems to be staying down. I must remember to thank him once my stomach and feet are on solid ground." She laid back and closed her eyes.

Hannah smiled and continued to read from where she had left off. After couple of chapters, she realized Sarah was asleep. She carried the tray to the door to discover a fresh bucket of water beside a wooden tray of cooked fish, cheese and ale. She had no idea what time of day it was, but the smell of the food made her stomach growl with hunger when she placed it on the table. She must find Thomas to thank him for the sending the food. She was grateful for the fresh fish. It was moist, well cooked, no hint of the offensive smell that she remembered from the dock.

Afternoon passed, Sarah continued to sleep showing no signs of distress. Hannah read until the light in the room faded. The swaying motion of the ship lulled her into a relaxed state of quiet contentment.

Sarah stirred in the bed. "I am going to live."

"Of course you are going to live. Do not think I am going to your mother and tell her you died your first day away from her, with sea sickness of all things." Hannah laughed at the thought of facing Ann, the only person she knew who could send the maids scurrying with just a look. "I would never be brave enough to face your mother with ill news." She took Sarah's hand in hers. "I am most happy you are back amongst the living."

Hannah pulled a fresh change of clothes out of Sarah's bag and discovered yet another bucket of fresh water sitting in the doorway. She carried it in and sat it beside the bed. "Are you feeling well enough to bathe?"

Sarah stood holding onto the bed. "I am."

"Good, because you smell dreadful."

"I can manage on my own. Go, go find that husband of yours."

Hannah smiled at Sarah and left her to make her way up to the deck. The cool evening sea air was a refreshing welcome respite from the stale, dank, confines of the sick room below. Testing her sea legs, she discovered she had little trouble walking on the ever—moving deck. The sails were full, making a slapping noise in the wind. She searched for Thomas amid sailors going about their duties, while others were relaxing in small groups about the ship. He was not on deck. Closing her eyes, she turned her face to the sun, low in the western sky.

"How is the maid, Sarah, faring?" William joined her.

"Much improved. Thank you for asking." Hannah smiled up at him.

"That is good. Would you care to join me for some ale and perhaps a bite to eat?"

"Yes, I would."

William took her by the elbow and walked her to the same barrel they had shared the evening before. He poured the ale for her, and removed the dirk from his belt making small work of slicing the cheese and dried beef.

She drank deeply. "You know this is my first time aboard a ship. It is nothing like the barges in London. I do believe I am enjoying sailing for the most part. The air is so clean and fresh. The motion of the ship cutting through the water is a challenge; however I am able to move about with little effort."

"Then you remembered what I told you about keeping food in your stomach."

"How could I forget? Every time I see you, you are feeding me!" She laughed shaking her head. "Sarah tried, but to no avail."

The two were quiet for a few moments. He watched her. "I am glad you have taken a liking to the sea. It is one of my favorite places. The Greeks say that Poseidon rules the oceans."

"I remember reading of him in Father's books." She was surprised William knew of such things. "Do you sail often?"

"As often as your father will allow. My father was a fisherman. I grew up aboard his ship. For me being at sea is the nearest thing to going home."

"I never knew." She shook her head when he offered her more beef. "I have known you my whole life. This is the first time I recall you ever mentioning your family."

"Your father keeps me too busy for social gatherings or being idle around the manor." He wiped bits of food from his knife and replaced the blade at his waist. "Let me share something else with you, it is truly wondrous." He smiled and guided her to the opposite side of the ship.

"Just there." He pointed to the sun when they reached the railing.

Standing there, she discovered a beauty never to be seen on land. She watched the sun reflecting off the water, glistening as if the Gods had sprinkled precious gems over the ocean. On the horizon, the sun slid to the water's edge. Above, small puffy clouds of pink changed into a kaleidoscope of color. Amazement filled her and she watched while the magnificent display before her faded to purple, blue and then grey. In that moment, Hannah found the meaning of contentment. A joy inside her that had nothing to do with elegant dresses, jewelry, money or even love. She discovered beauty and comfort in life's gifts, the motion of the ship, and the salt she could taste on her lips, while the display of color was a delicacy to her eyes.

"This… this is breathtaking. I have no words." Her eyes fixed on the horizon. "Thank you William." She absorbed everything around her.

"You are welcome Hannah. Now, I will see you back to your door. Sailors are an unpredictable lot. They can become most raucous after sundown."

They turned away from the railing. Hannah's eyes scanned the deck for Thomas. "Have you seen Thomas?"

"When the card game broke up he went below. That was…an hour or so ago."

She stopped at the steps. "I can make it from here." Puzzled she turned to face him. "William, where do you sleep?"

"I sleep under the stars, just over there," he indicated and chuckled. "It is the best spot on this ship."

"Oh."

"Don't look so shocked. I enjoy it. Except, when it rains, things get slimy when there is rain." He laughed.

Hannah smiled at him. "Thank you again, William, for sharing the sunset with me. I have never seen such splendor." She turned, walking down the steps. Pausing at the bottom, she looked up, he was gone.

She walked the short distance to her cabin, stopped outside her room. There was no sound of Sarah being ill, so she continued down into the hold of the ship in search of Thomas. Crates formed walls around her when she reached the bottom of the steps and pale light spilled down the from above. She could go no further. With a hand on a huge crate, she blinked waiting for her eyes to adjust to the darkness.

Great sacks, heavy with their contents swayed to the rhythm of the ship, and the timbers making up the sides of the vessel creaked. Water slapped them on the outside while the rattle of barrel contents added to the cacophony that assaulted her ears. Musky, damp odors filled her nose. A rat scurried into the gloom. Taking small steps, she edged forward. The ship lurched throwing her into a gap between the crates. Landing face down in the tight area, she pushed herself up onto her feet. Voices came from the other side of a large box. She patted her hair into place and put on her brightest smile.

"Thomas, are you there?" She stepped around the corner. Her heart stopped. She inhaled sharply as her hands flew up to cover her mouth at the sight before her. Horrified she cried out.

"No!"

Chapter Seven

Naked, Thomas leapt from the pallet on the floor, crossing the small space in one long stride, his manhood stood stiff in front of him. He pulled Hannah to him. She stood there in shock, a look of horror and betrayal on her face.

"Phillip, leave us!" Thomas commanded with unholy calm while his eyes bore daggers into hers.

Phillip sat unruffled, naked on the rumpled blankets. His face was void of all emotion. Taking his time, he pulled on a pair of breeches and slipped his shirt over his head. With a half—smile thrown in her direction, he left the area.

"How dare you spy on me?" Rage engulfed Thomas's face, the red spreading down his neck. The veins across his forehead bulged.

"I, I—" her voice just above a whisper.

"You did not have my permission to enter the hold. I left you in your cabin." He slapped her face.

Her eyes watered, the back of his hand struck another blow to the other side of her face. "You are now my wife. That makes me your lord and master, you stupid little fool." He threw her into a crate.

She melted into a heap on the floor. Her forehead hit something solid. Blood ran into her eyes, her face on fire from his blows. The hold whirled. Little silver stars sparkled on the outer edges of her vision.

"Madam, I demand you to get up."

With both hands, she tried to push herself up. Shaking with fear, she fell back onto the floor. "I…I cannot," she whispered.

Thomas grabbed a handful of her hair, pulled her to her feet, and then he threw her against the hull. Her head crashed hard against the solid oak, and her vision grew dark. His fist slammed into her face. Both lips split; the metallic taste of blood filled her mouth. She managed to remain on her feet by clinging to a short barrel beside her. She tried to focus, the cramped area continued to swirl.

"What do you have to say for yourself, madam?" His face inches away from hers.

She spat the words mixed with blood. "Me? You are an abomination before God."

Again, he threw her, she landed on the make shift bed. He forced her face down into the coarse blankets. The bed smelled of unwashed male, sweat, and damp wool. Her stomach lurched. She was going to vomit. She attempted to struggle away from him. She felt her petticoat and skirt jerked up over the back of her head.

"You want bedded? Well, madam, you are going to get what you want," he snarled in her ear, spittle dripped onto her face. "Our marriage will be consummated here and now."

With one hand on the back of her neck, forcing her face further into the bedding, he ripped her small clothes from her lower body, forced her legs apart with his own and shoved himself inside her. Searing pain tore through her body, her attempts to scream, lost in the depths of the blankets. He thrust into her again and again. Her delicate flesh tore. Her mind went blank, her breath stopped. She was going to die. Her hands flailed, trying to grasp onto anything, there was only the bloody blanket beneath her face. Her lungs were desperate for a breath. He jerked her head backward. Her lungs fill with the putrid air. He ripped hair from her scalp and slammed into her once more and she felt his body spasm.

"There, it is done." He breathed heavily for a moment and rolled her onto her back.

"My father will hear of this." Gasping, she spat in his face.

"You are no longer your father's concern. You are my lawful wife. Wedded and bedded." His face contorted. "Mine to do with as I see fit."

Hannah slapped his demented face with every ounce of her remaining strength. Unfazed he pulled her to her feet by her shoulders and threw her once again against the hull. She slid down and he pinned her. Thomas punched her in the face. The stars exploded and her sight went black for a moment. She opened her mouth to scream, but was cut short by his hand around her throat. Tighter and tighter it squeezed, her vision darkened. Her heart pounded in her head, like the blacksmith's hammer striking an anvil. She attempted to hit and kick, but her strength had abandoned her. Her life slipping away. Thomas's hideous laughter filled her ears.

Her hand struck a flat, sharp and cold object on the small barrel. The blade cut into her fingers when they wrapped around it. Her eyes would not focus; all she could make out was a red-eyed demon with a distorted mouth in front of her. Without conscious thought, her hand sought the handle of the knife. Once found her fingers grasped the handle and her arm came up. She struck at the demon. She struck out, once, twice, and drifted on the edge darkness.

Thomas fell away from her. She drank in the precious oxygen and fought to remain conscious. The ship pitched and she fell forward landing on top of him. The knife sank into his flesh. Blood poured out of his body.

Help, I have to get help.

Pushing herself up, she crawled across the floor. Groping at the hull, she found a crate, and used it to pull herself upright.

With trembling, bloody hands, she felt her way around. Stumbling and weak she found the steps. Hannah tried to call out. Her throat burned, unable to produce a sound. Falling against the rough stairs, she crawled up. Her kirtle tangled with her feet, she heard the fabric tearing. She advanced with slow, painful movements. Once she made the landing, she attempted a gain to call out. She managed a strangled gurgle. Groping the wall, she found the latch to her door and pulled herself up. She fell against the door, it flew open and she crumpled onto the floor.

A face floated above her. With a hoarse whisper she managed, "Find William… on deck." She succumbed to the blackness.

Chapter Eight

William stood on the forecastle beside a giant of a man, his large arms crossed over his barrel—sized chest. Long curls of light auburn hair tied with a strip of leather at the base of his neck while a bush of red beard reached to his chest. Rory towered over William. They spoke in hushed tones.

"We'll dock in less than two hours, according to the captain." William informed Rory who was standing in shadows.

"It will take several more for the ship to be unloaded," Rory said.

"I must continue on with the newly married couple. That is how Edward wishes this to proceed." He paused taking a deep breath. "Rory that is why I need you to be ready for a quick departure when the planks touch the dock. Even though Protestants are returning to England, the Queen's life is still in danger."

"Aye, I have word Francis Walsingham has left France to join her. In addition, the Pope has sent letters to her with threats of ex-communication. He has even threatened to order all Catholic subjects in England to disobey her. This may not be his only attempt at Papal intimidation."

"We must not fail. She shall need all the support we can master. En route to London, Francis will meet with Edward. There should be information coming to us from their meeting in the next broadsheets. We have much to do before we arrive home."

"Aye, it will be good to see Ireland again," Rory nodded.

William smiled. "Is it Ireland or Betsy?"

"Both. It is not good for a man to be away from his wife for so long." He looked down. "She will want to have another bairn by now."

"I am sure you'll be up for it," William teased, smiling, until he saw Sarah reach the top of the steps. The fear on her pale face showed in the soft light from the lamps hanging around the deck. "Something is not right."

Sarah spotted him, meeting him halfway across the deck. Her voice was just above a murmur. "Come quickly, it's Hannah."

She led the way back to her shared room. Hannah was laying on the floor, moaning each time she exhaled. William knelt beside her. Both of her lips split and swollen, ugly red welts circled her throat. Her left eye was swollen shut. He brushed hair away from her face to discover a small cut still bleeding above her eye. His jaw clenched, he looked up at Sarah. "What in the bloody hell happened to her?"

"I don't know, sir." Tears filled Sarah's eyes, her hands shaking. "She was only awake long enough to ask for you."

"Hannah," William lifted her with ease from the floor and laid her on the bed. "Hannah, wake up." He shook her with great care by the shoulders. "Hannah, it is William. What has happened? Who did this to you?"

"Thomas. I think I killed him…down below," she whispered before she fainted.

Sarah inhaled sharply and sank onto her knees.

William stiffened, clenching his jaw. His hand went to the bolster of his blade. Rage surged through him at the sight of her wounds. Using every ounce of self-control he had, he turned to Sarah. "Take care of her. Get her out of these clothes. Do not let anyone into this room. If what she said about killing him is fact, both of you are in danger. I will be back after I sort this out."

He left closing the door with a faint click. His footfalls did not make a sound stepping down into the black hold. Every muscle in his body taut, his breath quickened with each step. William's hand grasped the blade at his side waiting for his eyes to adjust. He turned first one way, then another. A cat stalking its prey. He climbed on top of a crate for a better view. On his right, Thomas lay naked on the floor, blood pooled around him.

William dropped to the wood planks, bent over, laying a hand on Thomas's chest. There was no movement. With his teeth clenched, his tone was cold, "Death is too good for you after what you have done. I would not have let you die." He pulled the knife out of Thomas's side. Removing a blanket from the make shift bed. The motion of the ship assisted him to roll the body with the knife onto the blood-smeared

cloth. He created a tight cocoon. Then picked up a shirt laying on the
floor, tore it into strips, and bound the blanket to the corpse.

See my daughter safely to France. Edward's words ran through his head.
Think, William, think. He had to come up with a plan. He must cover up
tonight's deeds and keep the women safe. There had to be a way. He
would get the women off the ship. Their lives depended on this, but
where could he take them? Many years had passed since he had been to
France. A plan began to formulate. He headed to the deck.

Rory remained where William had last seen him.

"Change of plans," William looked aft and then forward to the lights
on the dock. "There will be four of us going ashore. We'll need to get
off first and fast without being seen."

"We will need a diversion." Rory stated.

"I will get the boy to take care of that. I need you to rearrange
some of the cargo to conceal a problem you will find in the hold. It is
on the floor. It needs to be the last thing they uncover when the crates
are unloaded. Then meet me in Hannah's room. We will have to move
quickly, and split up as soon as we sit foot on the dock. Go to Louise's
place, take the long way."

They began to stroll across the deck, showing no signs of anything
being amiss.

Rory smiled at William. "You never do things the easy way." He
headed to the steps of the hold.

William continued around to the bottom of the ratlines where the
young men and boys were huddled together for a game of Fox and Geese.
A small boy watched his approach and disengaged himself from the
game. William put an arm around the boy's shoulders, steering him away.

One of the older boys called after them, "Where are you going
Gavin? We are winning."

William leaned over him whispering.

Gavin nodded with a frown.

William patted his back, "Can you do this?"

"Yes, sir," he replied.

"Good. Confusion will follow, and then I want you to slip off the
ship. Get away from the dock, and hide. Come morning, go to Louise.
I will meet you there." William handed him three pennies and headed
for Sarah.

Chapter Nine

The candles cast haunting shadows about the room. Sarah sat on the edge of the bed cleaning Hannah's wounds. Boards creaked, and moaned, the motion of the ship threatened to unseat her from the thin mattress. Hot and humid, sweat beaded on her face. Never, in her life, had fear engrossed her like it did now. Startled by a knock on the door, she dropped the wet, bloody cloth, and her hand jerked to her mouth to stop a scream.

"It is William. Open the door, Sarah."

Sarah let him in. Hannah remained on the bed with blankets up to her chin, unmoving. The only sign of life was a low whimper.

"How is she?" William asked.

"She is alive. There will be a scar just above her eye." Sarah picked up the torn, bloody clothes. Tears rolled down her face. "These are beyond repair."

"Sarah, I need you to listen to me." William took the clothes. "You have to be strong, do you understand?"

Sarah sniffled, took a deep breath, "Yes sir."

"We have to get off this ship," William stated.

"Then, it is true. Thomas is dead." She dropped to the bed, staring at the floor.

"Yes, he is dead. Only Hannah can tell us the why and how of his death. From the look of her and his body, something went wrong in a most horrible way. Regardless of what has happened this night, no one will believe the story of two women. He was, after all, her husband. Being her handmaid puts you in the same danger. We have to get somewhere safe and get you both back to England. You must do exactly what I say. There is no time for explanations. With luck, we might pull this off." He grasped her by the shoulders, forcing her to her feet.

She nodded.

They heard a tap on the door. Sarah froze.

William pushed her behind him, using his body to shield her. He opened the plank door slowly.

Gavin stood in the opening holding a cloth bundle.

William took it and handed him the bloody clothes. "Well done. You know what to do with these, and I will see you after."

Gavin smiled, nodded, and disappeared.

After closing the door, William tossed the bundle on the bed. "Help me put these on her."

"I do not understand?" Sarah stood. He had gone mad. What was he thinking? She would not dress Hannah in wool breeches, and a leather jerkin. This was unheard of.

"They will be looking for two women leaving the ship, not two *boys*. We have to work quickly. There is no time for modesty." He pulled the blankets from Hannah.

They worked without speaking, dressing Hannah in grey breeches and a dirty, tan jerkin. She moaned on occasion, but never opened her eyes or protested. Soon, she was dressed. Hannah was transformed into a boy of eleven or twelve years of age, and sitting on the bed, slumped forward. The worn, soiled jerkin was large, concealing all signs of her breasts. The sleeves of the under shirt hid the soft, feminine arms inside.

William grabbed a flagon of wine, took a drink, and poured some on the front of Hannah's jerkin.

Sarah started to protest. William appeared to know what he was doing. She watched him in silence.

"Can you get her hair under the cap somehow?" he asked, finishing off the flagon.

"Yes sir." She produced a comb and set to work at the task. Grateful to have something to do. Fear knotted her stomach. The motion of the ship no longer made her ill, but she hated sailing. Should they escape, unhindered, to England, she would never leave dry land again.

Her fingers toiled with swiftness braiding Hannah's hair in tight rows close to the scalp. She pulled the black wool cap down over the braids and stood back.

"Well done, Sarah. Now you must also get changed." William indicated the other half of the bundle.

"Sir?" Her eyes widened.

"If you insist on modesty, I will keep my back turned." He turned to face the door. "Hurry Sarah, we do not have much time. Remember to hide your hair, also."

Sarah obeyed, in silence. Tears filled her eyes. This was no time for weeping. There was an urgency in his voice encouraging her to action. Soon she whispered, "Sir, I am ready," while she twisted her hair into a knot, pulled the cap over her head.

William reached into the lamp globe hanging from the plank ceiling and ran his fingers across the soot. He turned and smeared it over Sarah's face, neck and hands.

"If you are to be boys, you must look like boys." He proceeded to Hannah's face.

There was a firm knock on the door. He pulled it open enough to see Rory, and then dragged it wide. His bulk filled the majority of the room. Sarah drew in her breath sharply and backed herself into the corner.

"Sarah, this is my associate, Rory. He is going to help us get off the ship and away from the docks."

Rory inclined his head to her and then looked to William. "It is time."

William turned to Sarah, "All you have to do is stay beside Rory and be silent. Not a word, do you understand?"

Sarah nodded and stepped to Rory. William then spilled a small amount of the wine cask on Sarah clothes. Setting the jug aside, he turned and blew out the candles, engulfing the four in darkness. William and Rory held Hannah up between them, and they all left the room, closing the door behind them. Sarah walked close beside Rory.

On deck, Sarah watched a flurry of activity, men bustling about preparing wooden barrels for unloading. The rank smell of dead fish mixed with recent dumped chamber pots, assaulted her nose. The coolness of the air, mixed with the sweat on her skin, causing goose flesh, and shivers to run down her spine.

Between them, William and Rory half dragged, half-carried Hannah's limp body which showed no signs of life. Sailors yelled and cursed going about their work. None gave them a second look while they made their way, in the dim, across the deck.

"Do not see us," Sarah mouthed repeatedly as she remained beside Rory.

Her breath coming faster and faster, the gangplank appeared directly ahead of them. Footfalls sounded like horses stamping. Still she walked, keeping up Rory's pace.

They were mere yards from the plank leading to the dock, when a man appeared stepped from the shadows. "Hey mates, where do you think you're going? Why are you carrying that lad?"

"The two of them got into my wine cask, ended up drunk and in a fight. We're helping them walk it off before we deliver them to their mother." The words slid off William's tongue like honey, while Sarah lowered her head and held her breath.

The man stepped up to Hannah lifting her head with a large meaty paw. He turned it one way and then another.

A smile spread across his face. "Looks like you got the worst of it, lad." Then, he turned to Sarah, "Did you do this boy?"

Rory elbowed Sarah hard on her shoulder. "Answer the man, boy."

Sarah nodded vigorously without a word.

"Help, fire. Fire down below," a loud, shrill voice shouted from behind.

The sailor's head whipped about, and he headed in the direction of the commotion. Sarah turned. Gavin stood across the deck at the top of the steps above the hold, smoke boiled behind him. He had the attention of every soul on board, men rushed to him. The ship's deck was in total confusion. Rory grabbed Sarah by the shirtfront, pulling her along, forcing her to quicken the pace.

William and Rory lifted Hannah up between them. Her feet just off the deck; the three of them ran down the plank to the dock. Sarah struggled to keep up. She feared if she stumbled, Rory's grip would force her onward, dragging her behind him. They ran until Sarah thought her chest would burst, and her legs fail. Once they were past the dock on a wide street, Rory released his grip on her shirt.

The stench of the harbor faded as their pace slowed to a quick stride. Rory took Sarah's elbow with a firm grip and guided her away from William and Hannah. The last she saw of them over her shoulder in the pre-dawn light, was William lifting Hannah in his arms, carrying her around the corner of a building.

"Do not be scared, colleen, I will not harm you, nor will I allow any other to bring you harm. From here, we are just a father and son out for an early morning walk. We will join them soon." Rory slowed their pace and led them down the cobblestone street.

She was grateful that he did not ask her any questions that required answers, for she did not think she could find her voice. Her breath was returning to normal. This was not what her mother had meant when talking to her about learning new ways. Not knowing why, she believed what Rory said about no harm coming to her as they walked. Frightened out of her wits, she believed that she would see Hannah again. What she did not know was what was to become of them once they were reunited.

Her breath calmed, "Where are we going?"

"To the house of a fine lady, although…I do not suppose you should mention being there to your parents. It is not the type of house, a colleen, such as you, would frequent. Should you ever have the pleasure of meeting my Betsy, you would do best not mentioning it to her either."

She had more questions than answers, walking the predawn streets of a strange city in a foreign country with a man who was alien to her. Who the bloody hell is Louise? How had Hannah managed to murder Thomas? Where is Phillip? Questions with no plausible answers. The one foremost on her mind, what would the morrow bring?

Chapter Ten

In a narrow alley, full of shadows, Sarah and Rory arrived at their destination. A white-washed three-story building with a side entrance lit by a lamp hanging beside the door. An older boy dressed in livery met them. Holding a lamp, he led them up a narrow staircase to a top floor room. There, Hannah lay unmoving, on an overstuffed bed. Was Hannah dead?

"She fainted moments after we parted." William sat in a chair beside the bed. "Her hand was bleeding more than I knew. She stuffed it into the waist of her breeches. Hannah never said a word, never once complained. Now she sleeps."

There was a sadness in his voice and on his face, which Sarah had never seen before, something else as well. She let the thought go.

"I will stay with her, sir. And, if I may speak freely, you look like you need sleep." Sarah knelt beside the bed.

"I think we all do. Let us hope this night's labors will be worthwhile." He headed to the door. "Do you mind sharing the bed?"

"No, sir." She sat on the bed beside Hannah and looked for signs of life.

"Let me know if you need anything. I will not be far." William and Rory stepped out of the room and closed the door.

Sarah left the bed and crossed the floor to the window. The room was spacious more so than any in the English manor house. Fine woven rugs depicted intertwined vines and flowers in shades of green on a field of crimson covered the floor. A table in the corner covered with cloth of the same design. She trailed her fingers across the fabric and marveled at the delicate needlework. Three brass lamp stood tall between the bed and fireplace. Their light caused shadows to dance about the room.

Dawn crept across the sky. She found no joy in the start of a new day. A shiver ran up her spine. She pulled the heavy burgundy drapes closed, shutting out the sun.

Cold, hungry, and exhausted, she returned to the bed. Slipped under the blanket, careful not to disturb Hannah, and closed her eyes. Images of Hannah covered in blood, the rage on William's face and running until her chest hurt. She squeezed her eyes tight and forced them away. The muscles in her legs twitched. *Thomas is dead; Hannah wounded and helpless. Here I am dependent on two men, one a total stranger. Oh, Hannah, what have you done?*

Sarah slept.

She awoke to a knock and opened the polished wood door. Standing in the hallway, was a woman in an exquisite red brocade dress with a black silk bodice. Every strand of her raven hair combed in place. Never before had she seen a great lady with her face painted. Sarah was fascinated.

"Hello, my dear, you may call me Louise. I am the owner of this house. I thought the two of you would be hungry, so I brought a tray up. Plus, I wanted to meet you. Do you mind if I join you?" she asked with a thick French accent and then winked.

"Please, come in. I am Sarah, milady."

Louise entered and sat the tray on the table. "It is good to meet you." Her smile was genuine and kind.

Sarah moved to the drapes and pulled them open. Sunlight flooded the room.

"How is the little one doing?" Walking in, she peered down at Hannah. "Oh dear," she caught her breath, and with a gentle touch, brushed a strand of hair from Hannah's face.

"I think the pain is too much for her. I slept beside her, not once did she move," Sarah whispered.

"William said she was hurt. I never dreamed it was this bad. I will send my handmaid up with some things that will help. Let her sleep. It will be good for her." Louise turned, and looked Sarah over from head to toe. "I will send up a couple of night dresses as well."

Sarah caught a glimpse of a question on Louise's face, but said nothing.

"Please, sit." Louise indicated the matching chairs beside the table. "Shall we eat? I am ravenous."

They sat before the window. The sun streamed through diamond shaped panes, reflecting off the silver tray, sending rays of light across the room.

"So tell me, I must know, is wearing men's clothing comfortable?"

Louise asked with a mischievous smile.

"To be honest, yes. They are loose fitting, lighter, and I can breathe and move freely." Sarah did not feel embarrassed about her appearance with Louise.

"I have always thought they might be. I am not brave enough to give it a try," Louise laughed.

"But, these do have an odor." Sarah wrinkled her nose.

"What is the matter with me? My manners have escaped me. I will send the maids up with a tub for you to bathe and light the fireplace. There is nothing better to make you feel desirable than a good hot bath. I shall have your clothing cleaned also, my dear."

"But William does not want anyone to see us." Sarah tried hard not to come across as ungrateful.

"You forget, I have total command of my establishment." Louise tilted her head to one side and smiled. "Besides, my girls are most discreet. I will handle William."

"So…you have children?" She did not think a woman could have had children and still have such a thin waist.

She looked puzzled. "I think William has not clarified my house properly. Allow me. Children, no. I do have a son. You met him last night. He will be leaving soon to be fostered with his uncle and learn the ways of life at court." She smiled a proud mother's smile.

Sarah listened, fascinated by her French accent.

"My girls, they work for me. They provide, let us say, pleasure for gentlemen. Very wealthy, prominent, men who can afford the best. All others turned away at the door. Only the best for my girls."

Sarah understood, at least she thought she did, but, did not know how to respond. Never before had she participated in conversation of this topic. However, this information did explain Rory's curious words last evening not mentioning Louise to her mother or his wife. Perhaps she had been too frightened to understand much during their flight. Now, in safety, she was capable of clear thinking.

"I understand." Sarah glanced to the bed.

"This is a good life for my girls. We are far from the docks so deckhands do not come here. Even if they did, they could not afford my girls."

Sarah sensed pride in Louise's voice.

"They are free to leave whenever they wish. Which they do, they fall in love and marry men who can afford to provide them with the finer things in life. They become consorts to the most powerful men in France." Louise smiled wickedly. "Some have been given land and incomes." Louise pushed her chair back and stood.

"Alas, I must go. Thank you, for allowing me to share a meal with you. I hope we shall become good friends." Louise leaned over and kissed Sarah's cheeks.

"Thank you for your kindness and hospitality. You are a most gracious hostess."

After Louise left the room, Sarah felt a bit of the sunshine had gone with her. The time they shared was most agreeable. The thought of telling her mother she spent the first night in France in a house of ill fame, shared a meal with a harlot, a woman she truly liked, was inconceivable.

She understood William wanting her to return to England. Misgivings were creeping into her thoughts. If she returned, she would end up marrying one of the serving men at the manor or a tenant. Life for her would continue on, not unlike her mother's, serving others. If she was to stay with Hannah, she might have a chance for a better life. A life different from what she was accustomed. In addition, she could not accept the thought of leaving Hannah.

A knock on the door interrupted her musing. It was Louise's son and two maids carrying a bathing tub. One produced a small cauldron from the large pocket of her apron and handed it to Sarah.

"A little mugwort and other herbs are inside this bag," the girl explained. "When steeped in hot water and allowed to cool they make a poultice that will reduce swelling and help bruises fade."

"Thank you." Sarah held the bag to her nose. The pleasant smell of dried mint greeted her.

"Ma'am," she curtsied and left.

The boy lit the kindling in the fireplace, while the maid dragged the tub closer to the flames. More maids appeared carrying buckets of hot water. Sarah let them go about their duties; she liked being the one served over serving someone else.

Sarah tried to wake Hannah. She tempted her with food and bathing. Sarah talked in a soft voice, praised the rose scented soap Louise had provided them, and the sweet smelling oil added to the water. Hannah whimpered, and refused all and pulled away.

Sarah let her be, and undressed. She sank into the tub of warm water, took a deep breath, closed her eyes and laid her head against the side. Only then did she allow her own tears to flow. She had been strong for so long. Her strength ebbed into the water. Relaxing for a moment released all the emotions held at bay. She welcomed the release, and tears flowed in silence. Holding her breath, she plunged her head under the water. Coming up for air, she washed her hair, steadied her resolve and got out of the tub.

She was ready to face whatever the future held. After all, she was her mother's daughter and Ann was the strongest woman she knew. Ann was always prepared to face whatever challenge life might throw at her. In addition, she did so with dignity and a strength that Sarah admired. She must find a way to help Hannah explain what had transpired in the hold of the ship. Refreshed and determined, she slipped into a soft, clean nightdress.

Sarah sat on the bed and looked at Hannah's bruised and battered face. The cuts were healing, but there would be scars. They would be minimal and would fade with time. Hannah had always been a pampered and spoiled child. Never had she witnessed any type of violence. What would she be like once the physical wounds healed?

"Hannah, you must wake and talk." Sarah slapped Hannah's hand.

"You have to tell me what happened. How is it that Thomas is dead?"

Chapter Eleven

Darkness is a comfort. No one can see you, and you can see no one in return. Obscurity in all directions, a great void of nonexistence, no odor or sound, nothing to touch, no matter which way Hannah turned the blackness, was there. She was content to remain, floating. Drifting like a feather on the wisp of a breeze, in the shadows.

Alas, this was not meant continue, for a grey mist began to encroach into the darkness. Ghostly faces appeared. She attempted to focus, and they slipped away, twisted, dissolved, and turned into nothing. A voice called to her from far away. Called her name. It also faded. Somewhere deep in the recesses of her mind she remembered. Something she must do, and then the thought was gone. The never—ending abyss engulfed her, and she drifted away.

An elusive voice called and she turned. The voice sounded again, she searched. It was far away, yet familiar, she knew this person.

Someone called her name bringing the pain. No matter how hard she fought, the voice pulled her into the light.

"Hannah, you must wake." Someone slapped her hand.

She moaned and jerked her hand away. Her face hurt, neck and throat burned. Her whole body ached when she moved individual parts, taking a mental inventory of the areas she was intent on not moving again anytime soon. She could make out the voice over the pounding in her head. Yes, she knew the voice, but this meant she had left the comfort of blackness. In the sweet blackness, there was no pain and she wanted to return so the agony would stop.

"Hannah, open your eyes. You must wake. It is I, Sarah. You must open your eyes."

Hannah's eyelids fluttered. The light hurt her eyes, the air her throat. Movement pained her body.

"Sarah. Oh, Sarah." Her words were raspy and she began to weep as memories flooded back. Thomas, Phillip, and unbearable pain.

"There, there, poppet, you are safe. No one is going to hurt you." Sarah patted her hand. "Look around. We are not aboard the ship. You are in a soft warm bed. This is a fine house, on dry land, in France."

Hannah's tears exploded. The pain in her heart gave way and poured out. Her life would never be the same. She was betrayed, horrified, and defiled. She had committed murder. Her whole world destroyed, in one night. She wanted her father, and to go home. She wept, until there were no tears left.

"Do you remember what happened?"

She pulled away. "No. No, I cannot," she shook her head.

"You have to tell me what happened. I have to know."

"I cannot," Hannah whispered.

"No. You do not understand, you have to tell me. They are looking for us. We are in hiding, wanted for murder."

"What?" Confusion set in. "Who is looking for us?"

"First, tell me what happened and then I will explain."

Hannah breathed in deep, and swallowed hard.

She closed her eyes and shivered. "I found Thomas in the hold. He was naked in bed with Phillip. He ordered Phillip to leave, and he hit me. Thomas hurt me, he raped me, tried to kill me. There was a knife."

She shrieked. "Sarah, I killed him. The knife was in my hand, we fell. We were on the floor. The knife stuck in his side and he was not moving. The blood, there was so much blood."

Hannah pushed a coverlet to her face and screamed.

Sarah reached for her.

Hannah retreated further across the bed, screaming into the soft cloth. The painful memories were more than she could endure.

"I want my father. I want to go home. Take me home to Father." Hannah whimpered and collapsed back into the nothingness of the dark.

Chapter Twelve

"Those were her only words. She has not spoken since."

Sarah sat across the table from William in the scullery. The room was spotless and windowless. Wall sconces and the light from the next room filled the room drawing Sarah's attention to the shelves of porcelain dishes on the wall opposite of her. The scent of soap permeated the room.

"She sleeps now, not like she did before. It is a more natural sleep."

William's knuckles were white as he gripped his flagon of ale. "The bastard will never hurt her again." It was a statement. However, the anger in his face said more. "Death was too good for him."

"What do we do now, sir?" Sarah forced herself to calm.

"We must leave France. The authorities are looking for the two of you. My diversion did not go as I planned. Phillip has stated she was with Thomas prior to his death. They suspect she was not alone in killing him. The blood trail she left, led to your door. Both of you missing, it does not look good." He raised the flagon.

"How soon will she be able to travel?"

"She is strong and healthy, she will recover. She has full use of her fingers. Perhaps a day or maybe two." She watched him.

"I shall book our passage at the earliest possible opening. Hannah cannot return to England, she is a murderess. On the other hand, you will have to return and tell Edward everything. I will take Hannah to Ireland. I can keep her safe there until I receive word of how to proceed."

Returning to England alone, without Hannah she could not do, and had to come up with a way to convince William. She chose her words with care.

"Sir, when you asked about Hannah traveling, she will not be able to travel so distant. She is not strong enough for voyage. I did not realize you were speaking of going so far away."

Sarah did not look him in the face. Her stomach tightened. She had witnessed his anger and did not want to be the subject of his wrath.

"Her body is ready for travel. She will follow where she is lead, she will eat if you feed her like a child. But, her spirit is broken."

Keeping her head down she continued, "And sir, I mean no disrespect, I will not leave her."

"Bloody hell," he shouted, slamming his fist on the table.

She startled. "It is not her fault."

"I bloody well know that," he cut her off.

She felt his eyes on her. This was the first time she had been insubordinate and was prepared for the consequences. She would stand fast. She would not leave Hannah.

He took a deep breath. "I apologize. I know it is not her fault. When I think of what has happened to her." He walked to the door, not finishing.

She sat motionless watching him. He stood with his back to her. When he turned to her, his face was calm.

"We put Louise in danger. We cannot stay here." He paused. "I am going to leave for a couple of days. Rory will remain to watch over you. Make him a list of whatever you need to care for her. Have everything packed on the third night. We will move out then. Do not go outside, stay away from the windows. No one must see you. Can you do that?"

"Yes, of course." Sarah relaxed; he was not going to send her away. "Where are we going?"

"I am working on that. Remember both of you must be in breeches when we leave at midnight." He paused, looking into her eyes. "You can ride a horse? Like a man?"

"I can try, although I have never attempted to do so." She refused to tell him she had never been on a horse.

"Good. There will be no carriage or wagon. We carry what we need on horseback, and travel with haste. Rory will help you pack." He turned and left.

Chapter Thirteen

Hannah's silence continued. Her days spent in bed. Questions went unanswered. She had become a mere shell of her former self, while Sarah was lost in assisting her to return to the living. Nights filled with Rory vigilant and watchful outside their door. By day, he slept propped up against the wall next to their door. No one approached without his approval. Sarah was certain it was orders from William. She had not made a list for him, she only asked for a fresh change clothes for herself and Hannah, which was promptly delivered.

Louise came each day to share lunch. The two women became friends. Sarah would tell her of her life at the manor in England and she hung on every word, asking questions now and then. Louise would in turn tell her of the local gossip and of the French court. Sarah delighted in her mischievous smile when she spoke of the seedier parts. Sarah was saddened by the thought of leaving.

William, true to his word, arrived on the third night with four horses. He asked after Hannah's health.

"There has been no change, sir. The bruises are fading and the cuts healing. She has not spoken. I am at a loss for something to help her."

"You have done well. I am sure you have done all you can, Sarah. No one could ask for more. However, we must depart. I have found a place for us and give her time to mend. I swear to you, Hannah's recovery comes first."

"Thank you, sir".

"I will keep you both safe."

"I do not know what would have become of us if you had not been on the ship. I am grateful for all you have done."

William took her by the shoulder. "It is not yet over. We still have to escape the city. I am very proud of you. You must remain strong a little longer."

"Yes sir." Deep in her mind, a place where she pushed her fear, the horror of that last night on board ship lingered, threatening to surface. She could see herself giving in to hysteria. There was strength about William. She trusted him so far, though she feared where the morrow would find her.

They left the city by the dark of the moon. William held Hannah in the front of his saddle while Sarah rode beside Rory who led a packhorse. The sound of the horse's hooves drummed in her ears. She imagined danger around each turn and in every shadow. They rode without speaking.

Outside the city, William picked up the pace. He and Rory looked over their shoulder from time to time. Rory kept close watch on Sarah's ability to keep seated as they continued down the path. After several hours in the saddle, the inside of Sarah's thighs began to chafe and the reins were rubbing blisters on her fingers and palms. She admonished herself by thinking of all that Hannah had suffered at the hands of Thomas. Still, they could not ride forever.

How long would it take Hannah to regain her wits? Days, weeks, or months, Sarah did not have the answer. They had traveled for miles when William slowed their pace. He led them off the main road onto a trail that twisted back and forth through dense trees. The air was cool and crisp with a moist earthy smell. The trail narrowed forcing them to ride single file. Sarah saw the break of dawn, the sky turning from dark to grey and then to pale blue as the trail widened, allowing them to ride two abreast.

Sunlight poured over the hills revealing a quaint wattle and daub cottage in a hidden valley. The small building was sheltered behind large trees. A stream babbled to the right of the cottage. Small windows with wood shutters opened wide revealing the openings contained no glass. Smoke rose from the native stone chimney.

They rode to the side of the cottage, past a small neglected vegetable garden. William halted, jumped down from his mount and taking Hannah in his arms, carried her inside.

Sarah attempted to dismount only to find she had become stiff and could not complete the task. Rory was at her side, reached up, took her around the waist with his huge hands and set her, with ease, on the ground.

"You did a fine job, colleen." He nodded his approval.

"Thank you, Rory," she replied, stretched, and twisted, forcing her muscles to respond.

He took the reins of the four horses. "Off with you, I will be along in a moment."

Sarah headed to the cottage. Tired, thirsty, achy, and she smelled of horse. She did not care to ride again. This would be a perfect time for a long hot soak in Louise's tub. She was certain a French cottage would not hold such a luxury.

The back door was open and she heard voices upon her approach. She picked up her pace hopeful Hannah spoke to William. She entered and paused allowing her eyes to adjust. A fire burned in the stone fireplace, its light revealing a small kitchen furnished with a table and benches on either side. William was standing in a doorway opposite her and talked with the boy from the ship. They both turned when she entered the room.

"Sarah, I would like to introduce you to my ward, Gavin." William indicated the boy beside him.

Gavin lowered his head. "Ma'am."

"You are the one from the ship." Sarah was surprised.

"Yes, ma'am."

He could not be more than ten years old and was her size. His brown hair cropped short and the clothes her wore were similar to hers.

She turned to William. "You are the one who is responsible for the things we needed on the ship. All this time we thought it was ..."

"Yes, Gavin acted on my orders," William cut her off.

"Thank you, both of you," she said with heart-felt gratitude.

"You are welcome." Then to Gavin, he said, "Show Miss Sarah the house and where she can find Hannah. I am going to help Rory with the horses and bring in the supplies."

"This way, Miss Sarah." Gavin stepped aside so she could go through the doorway.

The cottage was a square, made up of four equal rooms, of all the same size. The inner walls were of wood, the floor was dirt, but fresh rushes had been scattered throughout. A kitchen, a sitting room and two bedrooms. She found Hannah in the sitting room in a chair beside the fireplace. The fireplace shared a chimney with the kitchen.

Sarah turned to Gavin. "Which bedroom may I take her to?"

"Master William said the one beside the kitchen is for the two of you, ma'am."

She nodded her head in dismissal.

Gavin turned heading to the kitchen. Sarah stepped closer to Hannah.

"Good morrow, I will get you something to eat and then help you to our room." There was no response. With a sigh, Sarah followed Gavin to the kitchen.

In the fireplace sat a black iron cooking pot of pottage sitting beside the fire. She had no trouble finding a wooden trencher and spooned out the mush, and returned to Hannah.

She ate less than half; Sarah finished off the remainder and returned to the kitchen. Gavin entered from the backdoor, arms laden with packages. He bowed his head and went through the opposite door. Rory followed his arms full of food supplies. Sarah ran forward to assist. "Here let me help."

Rory shook his head. "No, colleen, you take care of the wee one. You will both need some sleep, I expect."

"Thank you, Rory, you have been most kind."

Rory smiled and dumping his burden on the table. "I would like to think there would be someone to aid my Betsy, should the need arise, while I am away. Now off with you."

Sarah left him and led Hannah to their room. There she discovered a large package with her name written on an attached note. She unfolded the paper.

"Sweet Sarah, even though I envy you in your boy's clothing. I thought you might need these." Signed with a flourish - Louise.

Sarah unwrapped the package, finding it contained two off white night gowns, a blue and a brown outer woolen petticoat, and two matching wool bodices. Tears filled her eyes and her heart filled with gratitude.

"Hannah, look what Mistress Louise has sent us. She is very thoughtful, and generous."

Hannah stood before her saying nothing. Sarah took a deep breath and sighed. "I will help you change clothes and into bed. We both need sleep."

Sarah dressed them both in the new nightgowns and lay down beside Hannah. Looking around the room, she longed to be back with Louise. Here was a mere bed and chair. The bedding was grey wool. Cobwebs filled the corners. Sarah sighed, whispered a prayer for Hannah and another for Louise.

Her chafed thighs hurt and her back ached as she drifted asleep. She floated in and out of dreams. She was on horseback riding alone through the darkness. Someone was chasing her. She rode faster, and faster trying to escape, trying to find Hannah. In the darkness, she could not find her way. She was running through the cottage, running from room to room. Thomas was there, standing over Hannah with a knife in his hand. Blood everywhere, and Thomas was laughing, a hideous, evil laugh. Hannah lay on the floor dead. Sarah screamed.

"Sarah, you must wake. Sarah, wake now."

Sarah threw up her hands. "No."

"It is ok, you are safe. It is William. It was a nightmare."

Sarah opened her eyes. William stood over her, concern on his face. She sat up and began to cry.

"No one can harm you. I am in the other room and Rory is keeping watch in the yard." He turned and left the room.

She cried until there were no tears left. She slept a peaceful, dreamless sleep.

Chapter Fourteen

Hours became days. Days became weeks. Hannah's wounds healed, the swelling disappeared and her bruises faded. Hannah, herself, remained unchanged. Sarah watched William grow restless. Rory was absent for days at a time, and returned with fresh game. Sarah and Gavin carried out the daily chores of cooking and cleaning.

Each morning Sarah would dress Hannah and place her in a chair before the window in the kitchen while she prepared the food for the day. Sarah felt something amiss. She was wary and anxious. She tried to push the feeling away. William sat with her enjoying a flagon of ale.

Movement in the open window caught her attention. A cat leapt onto the windowsill. Grey and black striped, small boned and scruffy, the feline sat looking at them with quizzical green eyes. It looked at Hannah, tilting its head to one side. Then turned back to the two of them sitting at the table and jumped onto Hannah's lap. Sarah stood to shoo it away, William touched her sleeve stopping her.

"Wait," he whispered. "Let it be."

They watched the cat kneaded Hannah's lap, turn a full circle, and lay down. It began to purr. To the Sarah's amazement, Hannah raised her hand and stroked the cat. The purring grew louder and the cat closed both eyes snuggled down, curled its tail around and with eyes closed, kneaded Hannah's lap.

"It is reputed that Queen Elizabeth, when she was told of her sister's death said, *'this is the Lord's doing and it is marvelous in our eyes.'* I think that applies here," Sarah whispered to William.

He smiled. "This is marvelous, and gives me hope."

She frowned. "Perhaps I have done her a great injustice by aiding her too much."

"You may be correct. However, neither you nor I have dealt with a situation akin to this."

"I pray I have not delayed her recovery."

"Do not be hard on yourself Sarah. I think this may very well be the beginning of Hannah's return to us." He reached across the table and patted her hand. "Your mother would be proud of you, if she knew all you have done to help Hannah. I am proud of you."

Sarah blushed. "Thank you, sir."

***

Evening came; Hannah ate dinner with them in the kitchen without aid. The cat followed her every step and was in her lap whenever possible.

Hannah sat with the ball of fur while Sarah combed her hair. Candle light flickered and filled the room with the smell of melting tallow.

"What shall you call the little one?"

"I do not know." Hannah stroked the cat.

"Is it a boy or girl?" Sarah put the comb away.

No answer.

"Come to bed, you need to rest," Sarah said, turned down the blankets on the bed and blew out the candles.

Hannah moved, the cat jumped to the dirt floor, and followed. The two women settled into the bed. Sarah watched the feline wait for the movement under the blanket to cease, leapt onto Hannah's stomach and curled up.

She was fascinated with how attached it was to her mistress. She reached out to give the cat a scratch on its neck. Their eyes locked, the cat hissed before she made contact. She pulled her hand away with great care, mumbled to herself and turned her back to the cat.

Morning found Rory sitting at the kitchen table. There was a brace of rabbits on the far end and Gavin was making short work of skinning them. A pot of pottage was steaming in front of the fireplace.

"Good morrow, colleen," Rory smiled.

"Good morrow gentlemen," she replied. "Have I overslept?"

"Not at all, I had a bit of luck hunting, and the lad here is taking care of the fare." He took a huge drink from his flagon. "I hear the young miss is doing well."

"Yes, she is dressed and should be here in a moment." Sarah filled a trencher and poured a flagon of ale. "It is amazing that beast could bring her back to her senses."

"It is the first time I have seen William smile in many weeks." Rory observed.

"Where is Master William this morning?" She sat across from Rory.

She watched Gavin and Rory exchanged a look. "He went to the city," was all Rory said. His attention returned to the trencher in front of him.

The cat strutted into the kitchen, Hannah a step behind with a black, floor length, hooded cloak about her shoulders.

There was a shuffling of feet as Rory rose to his feet. Sarah rose to fill a trencher.

Hannah followed the cat in silence out the back door.

Sarah exchanged looks with Rory and Gavin. Panic filled her. "Where is she going?"

Rory shrugged, "I will look after her," and left.

Chapter Fifteen

Hannah followed the cat away from ever-watchful eyes, down a trail, not knowing where it would lead. The path wound uphill from the cottage. Above the tall trees shaded her. The air smelled fresh and clean with hint of damp earth. The sound of running water somewhere in front beckoned her. She continued and discovered a stream.

The tabby led her to a flat rock covered in thick moss. She sat, careful not to let her skirt trail into the pool below. She closed her eyes, listening to the rush of the stream making its way over rocks and boulders. Breathing in the damp air around her, she opened her eyes and looked up at the trees above. Their limbs moved gently and allowed the sunlight to flicker through to the ground below.

There was a sense of goodness and magic in the air. The warm, strength of the rock radiated through her body. A gentle breeze touched her cheek. Across the way, stood an ancient oak tree. It grew firm from snarled roots, thick as her body, twisting around the base and deep into the earth. Its trunk solid and unyielding, branches spread skyward like arms. Its leafy fingers reached to touch the sky.

Movement began, soft in the beginning. The wind caressing the leaves, the tree twitched, letting the essence of the breeze touch every part of its being. The current of air grew stronger, and stronger, playfully pushing the tree, until the tree began to sway. The wind and the oak, swaying back and forth, dancing together. Their dance changed tempo to the whim of the element from the east.

Hannah sat watching. The beat of her heart changed with the tempo of the dance. The power of the mighty oak surged, the wind increased. Her heart beat faster and tears filled her eyes. She cried, thankful to the life force of the tree. Like the oak, she too must bend to the dance of the winds of change. She must remain strong. The body would sometimes yield, but her spirit continued on, and would endure. She would find the perfect place to plant her own roots deep.

Standing, she wrapped her arms around her and swayed with the rhythm of the dance. She could bend, sway, and remain firm and whole. Her whole life lay ahead of her. All she had to do was find where she belonged. She took a deep breath. The cat looked up at her, mewed and headed down stream. Hannah followed with her mind cleared of the grey fog.

Chapter Sixteen

William stood on the deck of a Spanish galleon. His eyes took in everything, not one movement escaped.

"I am looking to book passage for five. My needs are simple, a cabin for my son and the woman who cares for him. She will see to his needs and they will not be a burden to you. The other two and I can sleep on deck."

The first mate looked hard at William, "What is wrong with your son? Not the pox?"

William smiled. "No, I assure you. A horse in a hunting accident crushed him. I have heard that Spanish doctors learned much from the Moors and are renowned for their cures. This is why we must get to Spain post haste."

The first mate nodded his head. "You have heard true. This is a wise choice for your son. However, do you have the agreed upon coin?"

William tossed him a purse. The first mate bounced it in his hand judging its weigh and then tucked it into his belt. "Very well, we sail for Spain two days hence, at dawn."

"Until then," William bowed his head, turned and left the ship.

William walked from the dock; making his way, turning this way and that down the streets that led into the city. He knew looks can be deceiving, he was an expert at making things appear unimportant when he was dead serious, and knew where to go, and what he would do once he arrived at his destination. He had been doing this sort of thing for many years, and was good at it because he was still alive. Today was no different. He needed information about the search for Hannah and Sarah. He knew the one place he could go to obtain the information without bringing unwanted attention.

William entered the tavern where the locals and a few sailors found their way at days end. At a glance the place did not look like much, almost neglected. There was a single wooden plank hanging in front with a crude painting of a white horse. William had been here years earlier; his mission was this evening was not so different.

He found a secluded empty table in an obscure corner. The lanterns hanging on either side of the table reflected dimly into the room. He ordered a tankard of ale and sat in the shadows, anyone looking his way would not be able to see his features, just an outline. With his back to the wall, he waited, watched and listened. Some sailors and a few locals began to drift in. Wenches with breasts spilling over the top of their bodices called to them from across the room.

He smiled; these were a lower class of working women, nowhere near the caliber of Louise's girls.

Off to his right, a couple of gaming tables were beginning to fill up with patrons. The men came here to drink and wench or to spend a few hours in male conversation before going home to their wives and families. These were the ones William would eaves drop on. The odor of their unwashed bodies assaulted his nose.

Luck was on his side; a constable walked in and joined two men at the table closest to him. William lowered his head letting his hat obscure his face further.

"Ah, to sit for a moment and rest my worn feet with a tankard in my hand is a great pleasure!" The rotund constable smiled at his companions.

"Don't tell me, you are still looking for those two English women," the first man said.

"Yes, I am. That young fop, Thomas Sollinger, has my superiors in an uproar. Demanding they be found. You would think he was searching for the Queen of England herself the way he is strutting about town. Now, he claims a man by the name of William may be involved. Says this William was also on the ship and he too disappeared. William, he says. Do you have any idea how many Williams there are in France? No surname just William." The constable shook his head and yelled for ale.

William leaned onto the table on his elbows. Thomas, he had said Thomas. That is impossible. Rory hid his dead body in the hold before we docked. He held his breath and listened. Anger flooded him as he thought of the possibility of Thomas walking and breathing.

"I think I saw him today," said the man.

"Oh yea," the constable laughed. "And which William would that be?"

"Not him. The fop looking for his wife, a tall, thin fellow. With dark hair and a dark beard. Not a hair out of place. He was dressed in expensive clothes and struts about as if he were at court. You know the kind, never done a day's work in his life. He carried a locket around with a Lady's portrait in it. He was offering a reward for information."

"That would be him. He wants the Lady beheaded for the murder of his friend. He claims she is his wife gone mad."

"She would have to be mad to have married Thomas Sollinger, he is well known in buggering society," the third man at the table spoke at last.

"He likes the young boys best I hear. Not a male bum is safe around him. You had best not turn your back to him, even if you find his wife." They laughed and the conversation turned to their families and friends.

William had heard all he needed. He slipped unseen from the tavern into the twilight and headed to the stable to retrieve his horse. He tossed the groom a coin and stepped into the saddle. His mind was churning.

Thomas is alive. Alternatively, had Phillip stepped into Thomas's place? That was the only clear explanation. He was certain Thomas was dead. He had seen him with his own eyes. On the other hand, the two of them were similar, Thomas and Phillip; they both were fair skinned, dark hair and beards. Both were tall, thin and of the same height and about the same age. If you described one, you described the other. It has to be Phillip. To what end? What could Phillip possibly gain?

William had gone to the tavern for answers, and now he had more questions. Panic caused him to tense - Hannah. He kicked his horse's sides and headed for the cottage.

"See my daughter safely to France." In order to keep her safe he had to get her out of France. "What am I going to tell Edward?"

Chapter Seventeen

On the morrow, Hannah and Sarah were in the kitchen making bread. The smell of yeast hung in the air. The tabby lay in the window basking in the sun. Wherever Hannah was, the cat was never far away. The two women looked at each other as they heard the sound of horse hoofs approaching.

"It must be William returning," Sarah said. "Leave it to a man to know when there it fresh bread on the hearth."

Moments later, he entered the kitchen with Rory and Gavin in tow.

"Good morrow, Ladies," he sat down at the table. "Would you join us, I have news."

Hannah could tell by the look on his face it was not good news.

Sarah poured ale for everyone. After they gathered around the table, all eyes on William, he began to tell them what he had discovered.

They listened, hung on his every word until he got to the part about Thomas and the French authorities searching for them.

Hannah turned pale. "Thomas is dead! I killed him. You saw, and you said you threw him overboard." She looked from William to Rory. "How can this be?"

"Hannah, remain calm. You must trust me. I do not think it is Thomas." His voice was soft and tender. "I want you to close your eyes, go head, close them, and listen."

She felt all eyes on her and she gave in and closed her eyes.

"Picture Thomas and Phillip standing side by side," William directed.

Pain crossed her face. She felt her heart quicken.

He gave her a moment and then described Thomas as the constable had. "Now open your eyes and tell me who I just described. Was it Thomas or Phillip?"

Confusion filled her. Her breath caught in her chest. Her eyes flew open. "Truly I do not know, it could have been either one." Her voice was a mere whisper.

"I think Phillip is posing as Thomas." William ran a hand through his hair. "I do not know to what end. I paid Louise a visit and she has heard the same. Thomas Sollinger is looking for his deranged wife, and creating quite a stink with the French authorities. He wants you beheaded for the murder of Phillip." He finished speaking and reached for his ale.

Hannah sat there pale, and panted with fear.

"What now, sir?" Sarah asked.

"I have booked passage on a ship bound for Spain. The first mate was most willing to give up his bed for the right amount of coin," he smiled.

"Once we reach Spain, we will make our way to Ireland. Phillip will think that you do not have the means to leave the city, let alone France. We leave here tomorrow night." William took another drink.

"Sarah, I know how difficult it is for you to sail. I think I have a ruse to cover both you and Hannah. The arrangements I made are for my injured son and the woman who cares for him. Louise has furnished you clothes." He turned to Hannah, "you will have to wear boy clothes until we reach Spain. Yes?"

"Yes," she said.

"Well done."

"My father will be worried. I must get word to him, though I do not know how." Hannah's eyes filled with tears.

William glanced at Rory and back to her "I sent word to him, weeks ago. I stated only you are both safe and with me."

He turned to Rory. "We will be taking the horses with us."

Rory nodded his head, "I think we should make sure we leave no sign of our stay here. Just a precaution, we do not know what lengths Phillip might go to."

"I agree. Gavin, you help the ladies pack." Hannah watched William's shoulders droop. "Pack up the foodstuff. The women must stay out of sight."

"Yes, sir." He disappeared through the door.

William watched him go, then laid his head on the rough wood table and slept.

Chapter Eighteen

Twilight approached, the women were in their room, trunks packed and nothing left to do but wait. Hannah held the tabby saying her good byes with tears rolling down her cheeks. The cat had come to her in a time of need and she did not want to abandon it. She had no choice.

A knock on the door forced her to realize the time to leave was at hand. Hannah wiped her eyes dry and nodded to Sarah to open the door.

Gavin stood there grinning from ear to ear with his hands behind his back. "Come in, Gavin," Sarah said as she stood aside.

"Milady, I have a gift for you," he announced to Hannah with his chest puffed out. His light brown curls tousled.

Hannah attempted to smile.

From behind his back, he produced a small wooden cage with a piece of wool blanket in the bottom. He sat it on the floor beside Hannah. "I do not know if cats get sea sickness, but I do not want it left behind. I made this for you. The cat can come with us, I already asked Master William." The boy was beaming.

"Oh thank you Gavin." Hannah grabbed the boy, and hugged him to her and began to cry anew.

"I thought it would make you happy. I did not mean to make you cry." Gavin's face filled with horror.

Hannah held him at arm's length and looked into his face. "Gavin, these are tears of happiness. Not all tears are of pain or sadness."

"Then you like it?" He looked up at her.

"Yes, I like it very much," Hannah picked up the cage. "You must show me how to work the door."

Gavin demonstrated how it worked and Hannah placed the tabby inside. The cat was most curious and inspected every inch of the cage. When she began pawing at Gavin through the wooden slats, Gavin laughed and stuck his finger into the cage.

Hannah watched, this was the first time she had seen the child play. It touched her heart that this cat had brought so much joy to them both.

"Gavin this is a most wondrous gift. Thank you." Hannah smiled down at the boy.

"You're welcome." Gavin stood and ran from the room, and into the kitchen where William and Rory sat talking. They both looked up as he entered.

Hannah watched with her hand over her mouth to hold back her giggles.

"What is it boy?" Rory asked.

"I don't understand women folk, they cry when they are sad or hurt and they cry when they say they are happy. It is just confusing." He ran outside leaving both men laughing in his wake.

"The boy is learning," Rory chuckled.

Chapter Nineteen

By the dark of the moon, they saddled up. William took the lead with Hannah dressed as a boy in the saddle in front of him. Sarah followed directly behind them in old woman's clothes. A dark hooded cloak engulfed her, hiding her face and hair. Gavin rode beside her as long as the trail would allow and Rory brought up the rear leading a packhorse with trunks and a most unhappy cat in tow.

Hannah turned to see the cottage fade into the darkness as they made their departure. It was a bittersweet leaving. Here she felt safe. Now they must leave the haven behind and travel into the unknown. She wondered what the next leg of their journey would bring to them. She knew that she was once again herself, but she never dreamed that they would be hiding as thieves in the night. She was not accustomed to being a part of danger.

William and Rory seemed to take it all in stride as if it was second nature. *What does William truly do for Father? What are they involved in?*

She had never thought to question either one of them. Now, everything was different. All she had thought about was getting married and being a wife. All women did this. She had always wanted to be like her mother.

What a mess she made of her life. She fell in love with the man of her dreams and murdered him. Now she was in hiding, wanted for murder. She had been so wrong about Thomas; wrong about so many things. William had saved her. Had saved Sarah also. How could she ever face her father?

She rode through the night sitting in front of William, his arm around her, holding her close; she took in the smell of him. She could feel his chest muscles against her back. He held her tightly, protectively. She closed her eyes and gently relaxed against him. She felt his strength. There was a knowing that enveloped her, a knowing that this was a man. A man that did not have to prove himself to anyone; a man who protected her and would continue to do so. He was gentle and hard at the same time. Confusion descended, she did not understand the feelings overwhelming her.

The motion of the horse and the cool night air forced her into the warmth of William's body; the scent of him and his arm around her lulled her to sleep.

William pulled on the reins. He turned the horse about. "We are moments from the docks. Sarah, you and Hannah are not to say a word. We will get you settled in to your cabin. Once we leave, bar the door the best you can. No one is to enter other than one of us. Do you understand?" Hannah nodded her head against his chest as Sarah answered through the darkness.

"The activity of making ready to sail should give us cover. We will take no chances. It is imperative that we draw no attention to ourselves." William paused.

"Once we are out to sea, we can relax but a little." William turned the horse down the road once more and they continued.

Hannah stiffened in the saddle in front of him. Fear swept over her. As if he knew, William wrapped his arm around her, holding her close. *All will be well,* she kept telling herself. *William knows what he is doing.*

They boarded the ship without incident. This one was larger than the last. But the odor of dead fish in the port remained the same. William carried Hannah to their quarters.

Not much larger than the one before Hannah noticed, but well maintained, the walls and floor were at least clean. The only light, a lantern hanging from the ceiling.

Rory and Gavin left them to see to the horses. William paced the floor of their room. Hannah sat on the edge of the bed holding the cage and watched the lamp swinging from the ceiling. Above loud thumps, footfalls and yelling seeped through. The cat peered through the wooden slats at her and meowed in a loud indignant voice. She had enough of her confines and wanted out.

"Lock this door. Do not open it unless Rory or I am on the other side," William instructed at last, and he left them.

Hannah could feel her tension growing. Her face was white with fear. Their ruse could be uncovered at any moment. She could see fear in Sarah's eyes.

Sarah fastened the latch and pulled the largest trunk across the floor against the door, and sat upon it.

"It will be alright," Hannah whispered. "We have made it this far."

Sarah stared at her, hands shaking. "I have never been so afraid. I thought that once you recovered, all would be well. I did not think ahead, of what would happen after."

"Sarah, stop. William knows what he is doing. I do not know how he knows what to do but he does. All we have to do is maintain this farce. Once we get to Spain, he will find us a way back home. We will be reunited with my father and your mother once again. We must trust William." Hannah was not sure whom she was trying to convince, Sarah or herself.

The terror raced through her, clawing up her spine. Gnawing, intertwining with her muscles, sweat beaded on her face and she felt the whole of her body tremble. Fighting her fear, she forced herself to focus on the cat.

Stop, she thought. *Find something to do.* The tabby clawed her finger, drawing blood.

"You are most demanding for attention for someone without a name." She peered into the cage, "I shall call you Freya."

The two women sat in fear of the unknown, not a tear shed. Hannah listened to the creaks and moans of the ship anticipating the moment the ship would shudder under the sails and carry them away from danger. They waited, alone in the semi-darkness with an angry cat.

Chapter Twenty

William stood in the pre-dawn shadows of the deck; his hat pulled down in front. He watched as three men walked up the gang plank.

The first mate met them before they stepped on the deck. "Sirs, what is your business here?"

One of the men flashed a paper, "We are searching all ships leaving port. We are looking for two young women escorted by a man. We require an immediate search of your ship."

The first mate blocked their way. "You will find no young women here. We have only one woman onboard. An old wise woman. She is caring for the son of a noble man who is seeking the doctors of Spain."

"You are certain of this?"

"Do you question my word?" The first mate pulled himself to his full height, looking down at the man.

"I told you, there is no way these women could afford to board a ship for Spain." The tallest man turned on the other two. "I am going home. This is useless."

He turned to the first mate "Thank you sir, your word is sufficient, God's speed to you."

They turned to leave, William let out his breath. He slipped unseen to a vantage point where he could watch the dock. He ignored the activity aboard and focused on all movement on the dock below. There he remained until the ship took wind and set sail.

Once underway he made his way below to the room that held the precious cargo. He paused before the door listening, hearing nothing he sat down with his back to the door and settled in. Sleep overcame him before his chin touched his chest.

Chapter Twenty-One

Hannah woke sweating in the stifling, humid heat of the mid-afternoon. Finding a rag, she washed herself from a bucket hanging in the corner. The motion of the ship gave her comfort in the knowing they had left France.

It was not possible for Thomas to be alive, she had felt the knife sink into his flesh; saw the blood pool on the floor. William was correct, it had to be Phillip impersonating Thomas. There was no other explanation. Why? She did not have the answer. She could not find any reason, even in a remote fashion that made any sense to her. She was nothing to him.

She froze. "I killed his lover. He wants revenge."

Once home, her father would take care of this. After all, she had only defended herself. He had attacked her. She had not intended to stab him. It had just happened. Father had many solicitors and a barrister who could clear her. It was just going to take time to get there. When I am home, I shall never make a mistake like this ever again.

"Did you say something?" Sarah was awake and headed for the piss pot.

"No. I must have been thinking out loud." Hannah began to dress. Amazed she could dress herself in breeches and a shirt. "How do you feel? You are not vomiting."

"I feel well." She smiled at Hannah. "But I do not think that Freya likes it here." She pointed under the bed.

Hannah knelt down to look. Freya had escaped her cage and curled up as far back under the bed as she could get. No amount of coaxing could budge her. Whenever Hannah reached for her a series of hissing and spitting would erupt. Hannah decided it was safer to leave Freya where she was rather than risk having her hands shredded. She placed a bowl of water under the bed just in case the cat was inclined to drink. She searched the floor for signs of cat dung, finding none she assisted Sarah in getting the bread and cheese from a basket. Hannah was pouring ale when there was a knock on the door. She held her breath.

Sarah stepped to the door. "Who is it?"

"William."

Sarah pulled the trunk from the door to admit him.

He entered, and his eyes scanned the room. Hannah had noticed him doing this before. She had once found it curious, but had come to accept it as one of his many ways. Today there was something else in his eyes.

"William, is something amiss?" Hannah stepped toward him, clasping her hands in front of her.

Sarah lit another lamp and sat on the edge of the bed.

"There is a ship on the horizon. She sets high in the water and will overtake us before sunset." His voice was quiet.

"Phillip," she whispered turning white.

"I think not," he shook his head. "It sails from the wrong direction. Perhaps, the captain is worried about pirates. Either way we must be prepared."

Hannah found her voice, "What would you have us do?"

"Our ruse must continue, remember you are my son and Sarah is here to care for you. Continue to dress as when we boarded."

Hannah's hand went to her hair, "Sarah, the hat."

Sarah snatched the hat from the floor and twisted Hannah's tresses onto the top of her head.

"What about the others?" Hannah pushed the hat on.

"Gavin will be along shortly. Rory will stay on deck and see to the horses, he will let us know what unfolds."

"So now we wait," Hannah sat on the bed. The groans of the ship grew louder.

"Yes we wait but, we must also prepare." William walked to the table and pulled array of weapons from his person, laying them out for the women to see. "Ladies, choose a weapon." He stood back for them to see.

Sarah's mouth flew open. Hannah stood, moved in slow motion, staring at the blades. Her hands trembled. This was unexpected.

"Why?" she looked to William.

"Every boy aspires to the day he receives his first sword, it is a rite of passage. He is no longer a mere child; he is one step closer to becoming a man." William grinned. "Since I do not have an arsenal in my pocket, these are the best I can do."

"Sir, you indicated both of us should choose," Sarah spoke.

"Not knowing the intentions of the ship overtaking us, I will not have you defenseless. I do not expect you to wield a blade, but those who do not, die just the same."

Sarah bowed her head. "Yes, sir."

Sarah swallowed hard nodding her head and stepped forward. Hannah watched her pick up a small slender knife, and held it before her face, the light reflected off the blade.

"That will do well tucked into your garter," William said taking the knife and reached down to grasp the hem of her skirt. Sarah jumped.

William stood and faced her. "Sarah, I am going to show you how to place it in your stocking so that you will not hurt yourself."

Sarah once again nodded her head. She pulled her skirt up and blushed as William tucked the blade between her garter and nether stocking. He then took her hand and put it on the wooden grip.

"You grasp it like this and pull it up thus, or the edge will cut you or your garter." He guided her hand. "Now you try."

Sarah did as instructed pulling the knife from her garter and then replacing it letting her skirt fall back into place. She stood stiff and lost her balance in the tossing of the ship. She grasped the wall and looked from William to Hannah.

"Well done." William then handed her another knife with a leather scabbard. "This one you will tuck into the waist of your skirt in the back." William turned her around and re-tied her skirt so that it held the knife secure to her back. "Your cloak will cover it so it will remain unseen."

Turning to Hannah he said, "You're next. Until he is older, my son would carry this rapier at his side on his belt. As a man would carry a sword." He slid the scabbard into her belt. "Now choose one that will fit into your boot."

Hannah reached for the nearest knife; she paused, turning her palm up. Her hand unsteady, she looked at the six red, raw, scars crisscrossing her palm and fingers.

"I can do this." She set her jaw with determination and grasped the handle. She willed her hand not to shake as once again she was taking up a knife to defend herself. This time she did so with perfect knowledge of what she was doing. William would not ask this of her if it was not essential. She slid the knife into place.

William bowed his head to her in approval. The remaining knives disappeared back into various hiding places on his body.

The ship lunged. Hannah lost her balance and was thrown against William's chest. William held her by her shoulders until she was steady on her feet.

She felt warmth flood her face and was quick to turn away.

"I must tell you, should the need arise for you to draw a blade, do not hesitate to use it in a lethal manner." She found the hardness in his voice disturbing.

"Yes, sir." Sarah went about breaking the bread.

Something was on the other side of the door scratching. In one swift movement, William blocked the doorway with his body and pulled the thin plank ajar.

"It is Gavin." They heard the boy speak, his voice above a whisper.

William opened the door.

"What news?" He closed the door after him.

"Pirate ship," the words spilled out. "Rory spoke to the First Mate. The captain cannot out maneuver it. He fears he took on too much cargo. He ordered the ship to change course, to head landward in hopes we might reach it before the ship overtakes us. Rory says it will not work. The wind changed and works against us. Rory says they will be alongside in less than an hour." Gavin stopped to breathe.

The two women sank onto the bed. They looked to William. He was calm and showed no emotion. Hannah reached for Sarah's hand. She held it tight, re—assuring herself that they would survive this also.

Freya came flying out from under the bed. Hannah startled as the cat leapt into Gavin's arms. Hannah ran to the wooden cage and opened it. Gavin showed no sign of moving other than to scratch the top of Freya's head. Together they placed the cat in her place of safety.

William stood staring at the floor. Turning to the women, he instructed them. "Stow everything away. Then you must return to your sick bed Hannah. Sarah will read to you. You must both remain calm. This may not be bad news."

He reached for the door. "Gavin stay here with them. I shall return." The door closed behind him before Hannah could protest.

Sarah sat at the table reading by the light of two candles. Hannah had taken up her role and lay on the bed. Gavin was sitting on the floor playing with Freya through the slats of her cage. For all appearances they were who they claimed to be.

Hannah willed herself to stay calm until they heard the first cannon fire. A small shriek escaped Sarah and the book slammed shut. Gavin stood and went to her. He put a protective arm around her shoulders and patted her arm.

"Please, please keep reading," Gavin pleaded.

Hannah saw the fear in his face. "Yes, read."

Sarah opened the book. It took her a moment to find the place where she had left off. Sarah swallowed some ale and read.

Hannah did her utmost to shut out the noise from above them. She could hear shouting and the sounds of many feet running across the deck. The sound of more cannon fire and the shouts grew louder and the ship lurched. Freya hissed and Hannah sat up in bed. Gavin remained beside Sarah and the three of them looked to the ceiling. Yells from above grew louder, yet she could not make out the words.

Boom!

The door burst open, pieces sent flying about the room. Hannah froze. Sarah ducked and screamed. Gavin fell backwards landing on the floor hard.

A huge hulk of a man stood in the doorway.

"Everyone on deck now!" His voice boomed at them.

Chapter Twenty-Two

Hannah kept her head down between Gavin and Sara as they pretended to assist her and emerged onto the deck. The rocking motion of the ship lessoned and she could hear the waves lapping against the hull. She slipped her arm around Sarah's waist, under the cloak, and wrapped her fingers around the handle of the knife.

"This way," Gavin led them.

In the fading daylight, Hannah stole a glace and spotted William and Rory standing by a group of sailors. Men with guns and swords pointed surrounded them. Gavin led them to stand beside William.

Hannah regarded William out of the corner of her eye. He never looked at her. His eyes fixed on the Captain, who was in deep conversation with his officers, they too held at sword point.

The moments passed. Hannah could not see what was happening from where she stood. Her hat blocked her view. She heard indistinct voices and footsteps. Her grip on Gavin tightened and her fear mounted. She dare not raise her head to see.

"What is happening?" she whispered.

"The Captain of the other ship is coming this way." Gavin spoke softly into Hannah's ear.

Hannah heard footsteps drew close. She stiffened and watched a pair of boots continue past them. Then they paused, turned back, and stopped almost in front of her. She swallowed hard and held her breath. Her feet shifted and the hardness of her knife pressed against her ankle. It gave her no comfort.

"I know your face sir." The male voice was hard.

"Aye," William responded.

"Colin! Take this man and all who are with him to my quarters. He is the most dangerous man on board." The man in the boots ordered.

Another man answered. "Yes sir."

The boots spoke with authority. "Put two guards outside the door, fully armed. No one enters no one leaves, no one but me. And search the hold."

"Yes sir."

A firm hand took her by the elbow.

"Head down and do not speak," William whispered in her ear.

She obeyed his words and they made their way across rough wood planks leading to the other ship. After a few steps, the strength left her knees and she faltered. William scooped her into his arms and carried her.

She heard the door slam and the metallic click of a lock. The sound of it frightened her to the point of trembling. William carried her to a bench in the corner. Sarah was at her side and the two women sat holding hands. Gavin came to them and sat on the floor in front of them facing the door while William paced. Rory appeared calm, found a chair, leaned back with his legs stretched out before him and closed his eyes. Hannah's heart pounded in her chest.

A large dirty window provided little light. A wood table stood in the center, upon it lay a map weighted down with a candlestick and a tankard. Several small chests lined the walls. Hannah looked away from the small cot attached to the far wall. It reminded her of another ship and another time.

Through the thin walls, came the sounds of cargo scraped across the floor and men shouted breaking the silence. The horses stomped and nickered. This went on for what seemed like hours to Hannah while she watched William pace.

She shifted her weight on the hard bench and released her grip on Sarah's hand. Her head down, she stared at the floor, every muscle tense with fear. What would become of them? This situation was not good. A shiver ran across the back of her neck.

There were voices just beyond the door followed by the sound of a key in the lock. All heads turned to the door. Rory sat upright, ready to pounce. William stood still, his hands on his hips.

A man entered followed by three others carrying their belongings from the other ship, along with a most unhappy Freya in her cage.

In the center of the room, William, his face hard and dangerous, confronted the lead man. The older man ignored him and with a motion of his head, the three men sat aside their burdens and left. The door closed behind them. He turned to William and the two men stared at one another, face to face toe to toe, only a few feet apart. Never had Hannah seen William look this formidable.

Her stomach tightened, and she held her breath. Her hand fell to her boot, the knife only inches from her fingertips.

The ship lurched into motion. As if this was a signal, the two men lunged at each other, hugged and slapped each other on the back.

"Charles, my friend, it is certainly good to see you." William held him at arm's length smiling.

"Liam, you are a hard man to find." Charles smiled back at him. "This is the fourth ship that we have intercepted searching for you."

Bewildered, she turned from the two men to Sarah and back again.

Rory stepped forward and held out his hand, "It is good to see a friendly face, even if it is one as ugly as yours."

The two of them clasped hands.

"Rory, it has been too long. When are you going to leave Liam and come make some honest coin with me?"

Shaking his head, Rory smiled.

"Received word from Edward and set sail immediately." Charles explained. "I have searched for you for weeks. This is the fourth ship we have boarded. I even have a package for his daughter. Liam, you do know where his daughter is?" He looked at Sarah.

"Hannah is here." William walked over to her and removed her hat.

"Captain Charles, may I present to you Edward's daughter, Mistress Hannah."

Hannah sat unmoving. Disbelief and confusion clouded her thoughts. "You know this pirate."

William took her by the hand and pulled her to her feet. She stood before Charles. The size of a tree trunk, he towered over her. His grey hair pulled back away from a face tanned and lined from too many hours in the sun. He had bad teeth under an unkempt mustache.

"Mistress Hannah, I am delighted." He bowed to her. "Your father will be most relieved."

"You know my father?" She was mystified.

"Milady, I have known your father many years." His smile was genuine and kind.

"You said you have a package for me?"

"Yes, milady." Charles walked to one of the trunks, flipped open the lid and produced a small flat bundle.

William stepped beside her as she took the package, ran her fingers across her father's wax seal, and fought back tears. Weak in spirit, and travel worn, she wanted nothing more than to be safe in her father's arms. Breaking the seal, she pulled the wrapper away to reveal a small book.

"Is there a letter inside?" There was urgency in William's voice.

Hannah flipped through the pages. "No."

"We are fleeing for our lives, and he sends you a book of prose?" He slammed his fist onto the table.

Hannah went back to the beginning of the book and turned the pages. After scanning several, she rotated it sideways. "Wait, there is something." She turned the book back around.

Smiling she glanced up at William, who turned to Rory. She watched an unspoken exchange between the two them.

"Gavin, let us see to the horses." Rory placed an arm around the boy's shoulders. The two left closing the door behind them.

"Now Hannah, what have you found?" William turned his full attention to her.

"I am not sure." She flipped to the first page. "I need more light."

Opening another chest Charles produced a tallow pillar candle. He affixed it to the candlestick and lit it with the flame from a nearby lantern.

William pulled a chair to the table and held it for her to sit.

With the book open, she pointed to two lines of letters scrawled across the inside cover. "Father wrote these letters. I would recognize his writing anywhere."

Towering over her, the two men followed her finger.

"It is nothing, jumbled letters." Charles shrugged.

Again, she smiled. "It is quite simple really. Simple, but brilliant. It is a cypher. Father was an excellent tutor, especially when it came to ancient Greek. I think the man's name was Polybius who designed this one. It only appears to be two lines of letters."

"And?" William knelt beside her.

"Normally you read from left to right, but if you read this top to bottom like this," she explained, tracing the letters with her finger. "It works well with two lines. Three is a little harder and more confusing to someone who does not understand what they are seeing." Using her finger, she pointed to the letters and read, "Go with William there is more."

"More? There is more what?" William demanded.

With great care, she turned the pages. On page four, she turned the book sideways. Pointing to the margin near the binding she read, "I will come to you when I am certain I am." She turned four more pages. "No longer being watched. I have met with." Four more pages, "Francis, he would have William go forth with." She flipped through. "Our original plans. Know I love." The last message, "you and know you are in safe hands."

Closing the book, she held it to her chest.

Father loves me still. He will come to me. I can go home. I have not disgraced him.

Her throat tightened. She closed her eyes and allowed tears to slide down her cheeks.

William stood, placed a hand on Hannah's shoulder. "No one is to speak of this. No one. The authorities still search for us."

Hannah swiped tears with the back of her hand. Sarah nodded and lowered her head in silence.

"Charles, set sail for home."

"We already have, Liam. That was our original destination. And the cargo we took aboard will come in most handy upon our arrival." Charles smiled.

Hannah found her voice along with questions. "What about the crew of the other ship? What happened to them? William, why does he call you Liam? And where is home?"

Charles smiled. "Not to worry milady, the crew is just fine. Since the Captain was shrewd enough not to resist our boarding, we simply took his sails and left him, his crew and the ship will make their way as best as they can. The current should carry them landward in a few days. Giving us enough time to be safely away." He bowed to her. "Liam, you will be pleased with the cargo. Cannon, shot, powder, and chains all resting below. In addition, a small chest of gold and silver coin that will provide anything else you might need in the future. Now I take my leave of you. I have duties. And ladies please make yourselves comfortable." He bowed again and left.

Hannah noticed the door was unlocked after it closed. She turned, "Why does he call you Liam?"

"It is Gaelic for William. I would think, you being a master of letters, you would have realized it is also the last four letters of William."

His jest angered her. "Do not toy with me." She shrugged his hand away she thought. "Father is coming for me. I shall be home soon. Then, I can face the consequences and move on."

He laughed. "The true Hannah has returned to us."

She sucked in her breath, pushed her shoulders back and spoke with calm. "Where are we going?"

"My home in Ireland." He made a formal bow and turned to leave, then paused, his voice void of all emotion. "Rory and Gavin will have finished checking on the horses. I will send the boy with food. The three of you can settle in. He will fetch anything you require. Get some sleep. No one will disturb you. You are safe here. However, you shall continue being my son outside of this room." He was gone.

Hannah regretted being angry with him. Had he not saved her in France? She smiled at the book in her hands.

Father would not be pleased with her for being cross with William, or Liam, or whatever his name was.

She should have asked about sending a message home, letting Father know she was safe.   Instead, she had allowed her anger to best her. She would apologize the next time she saw him. He would understand how tired and drained she was. She walked to the meager bed and lay down.

Her head ached and her mind would not be silent. Thoughts raced.

I want to go home. Father still loves me. Father will put everything right. Stop, I cannot handle these things now. I need rest.

She opened the book, read her father's message again, and then turned to the first poem. Hannah read a portion of the first poem. Physical and emotional exhaustion over took her. She drifted into dreams of the home. Her mother smiled, took up her brush. Hannah turned her back to her mother, leaned in and relaxed with each stroke of the brush.

The dream shifted. She was once again walking down the aisle of the little chapel on her father's arm toward her husband to be. His face was hidden in shadow. Father whispered, "This is the man of my choosing. Be not afraid little one."

Chapter Twenty-Three

William appeared in the doorway the next morning. His eyes raked the room and rested on the pallet on the floor where Gavin had spent the night just inside the door.

He smiled. "I trust you slept well?"

"Yes sir," Sarah responded. She was finishing the braid in Hannah's hair so it would fit under her hat.

"Good. I thought I might take my son and his keeper for a walk on the deck. Some fresh air might do him good."

"Sounds wonderful." Hannah stood and presented her sweetest smile. "But first, I must apologize for my harsh words of last evening. I am truly sorry, William."

"Hannah you are a remarkable woman, and I am most impressed with you after all you have been through. You have every right to be angry. Your entire world, turned upside down. But we must all remain ever watchful until we hear from Edward again."

Yes, her life had changed forever. She would never again see the world as she once had. Remarkable was not the word she would use to describe herself, but at least she would never be so blind about the ways of the world. It was not perfect and she recognized she still had a lot to learn.

"Thank you," she lowered her head.

William opened the door and stood to the side. "Shall we?"

Hannah pulled her hat on. "Yes please."

On deck, they walked a casual pace. Hannah beside William and Sarah close behind. The fresh salt air was an excellent reprieve from the time the women had spent cloistered below.

Hannah's mind filled with a multitude of questions for William. She was careful not to voice them where someone might over hear her. Her voice just above a whisper so William had to bend to her to hear, she began.

"Where are we headed? And how is it Father knows?"

"We are sailing to my home in county Wexford, Ireland. Your father was sending me there on business, when I was, shall we say, interrupted." William's voice was light and non-judgmental. "I was to see you safely delivered to France and then continue on. The message you found let me know that he expects me to proceed as planned, despite the interruption."

"I don't understand. What business are you to do for Father in Ireland?" Hannah shook her head as they walked.

"The Queen's business, your father believes now is the time to set in motion additional safe harbors for Queen Elizabeth's ships. On my land is a harbor with a quay hidden from the open sea. You have to know it is there in order to find it." William looked across the open sea.

She watched him. He cast his eyes to the horizon at something unseen to her.

"It has not been used in years. It sits neglected and is in need of rebuilding. Your father is financing the repairs of the quay so it may once again be useful for her majesties royal ships and others that support England. We, as well as others, believe the royal fleet is necessity for the survival of the Queen's reign." William took her elbow as they walked the perimeter of the deck.

"Your father is setting up alliances. The Queen must marry, and not knowing to whom, many allies must be in order. It is all very complicated. If she marries France, then we may be at war with Spain. If she marries Spain then there will be war with France. The Pope is a factor as well. Regardless, her loyal subjects must be prepared to defend her."

"Father never mentioned his involvement in the Queen's affairs. This sounds as if he is involved with all the whore-mongering of court." Hannah protested. "He has always detested court."

"To the public eye, yes, but there is more to it." He stopped and faced her. "Perhaps it is time you know your father is one of Walsingham's men." William gave her time to allow this to sink in.

"Walsingham has ended his exile and returned to England. A staunch protestant and he is working with Sir William Cecil on the Queen's behalf. There are many who do not believe that Elizabeth is the legitimate heir to the throne. Some believe her a heretic and want her cousin Mary as the anointed Queen of England as well as Scotland. Elizabeth's life is in danger along with the survival of England."

"So, you and Father are helping her through piracy?"

"We prefer the term profiteering, but yes that is what we do. It is what we have done ever since we learned of her sister's illness," William admitted. "And we shall continue to do everything in order to secure the throne for Elizabeth and for the country. Queen Mary left England bankrupt and there is no coin to defend her. This we shall remedy. We take from those who would cause harm and use the riches for defense."

Hannah was having trouble absorbing all of this. Never had she dreamed of her father's involvement in spying, piracy and espionage. She had never given much thought as to what William had done for her father; she only knew that he worked for him. She had assumed that it had something to do with managing of the tenant farms. But, now—there is so much more. "Why are you telling me all of this?"

"Hannah, how did you come to learn ciphers?" William looked into her face.

"It was a game really. At least father made it appear that way when I was learning to write. I was very young and would get bored practicing my letters. Father made it fun. It was like solving a puzzle in the beginning. Not until years later did I realize what those puzzles actually were." She remembered it all very well. "He said some day I would be heir to all he owned and he wanted me to be educated. My parents could never have another child. They would not have a son."

"I think that you can help us while we wait for him in Ireland."

"How can I help? I am wanted for murder in France and England as well." His words confused her.

"You can help, because you can read ciphers. I can show you more. The rest we shall figure out once we meet with your father in person." William tilted his head down, his eyes searching hers. There was something more in his face, she saw it but did not understand.

"Okay, I will help. You must tell me everything. What do I have to lose?"

They continued their walk in silence. Father was not coming for her as soon as she would like. She might as well find something to occupy her time. Perhaps this was a way for her to assist their beloved Queen. After all, women were as intelligent as men were. A knowing beam spread across her face.

We only allowed them to think they were in control. A woman's wiles could be a precarious achievement.

With the dawn's light on their backs, the small party arrived ashore in small rowboats. The quay was indeed in bad repair. Huge portions of rock had collapsed into the bay. Sea birds dove into the water and surfaced with their morning catch. Squawks and squeals filled the air. Standing upon the sound and solid rock part of the quay Hannah, with Sarah at her side, took in what lay inland before her while she waited for their belongings.

A forest of old trees provided a backdrop for the picturesque scene of several small thatch roofed cottages, all in good repair, and one appeared inhabited for smoke rose from the chimney and a well-kept vegetable garden lay to one side. A large rectangular building of native stone stood in the center of the cluster.

Hannah breathed deeply of the fresh air and was grateful the inlet did not smell of dead fish. The rich loam of the earth and decaying leaves carried on the breeze tugging at her hat. A red haired woman, followed by three small children, ran toward them. Rory dropped the bundle he carried and ran to meet the family. Hannah's heart warmed to see Rory take the woman in his arms swinging her around full circle, as they kissed.

Her hand went to her heart and she smiled. Remembering her ruse of being a boy and should not be appreciating the touching display, she forced her hands to her sides. Rory stood the woman back on her feet and picked up all three red headed children. Squeals of "Da, Da!" reached her ears and Hannah's eyes welled with tears. She longed to be in the comfort of her father's arms. Only a short time ago she, herself knew what it felt like to be in the arms of the man she loved.

"That is true love," Sarah stated softly.

"I wouldn't know." Hannah turned away from the bittersweet homecoming.

"That is Betsy and the bairns." William indicated with a nod of his head they should follow him to the large building. They fell into step behind him and Gavin trailed behind.

The main structure, a large hall with a fireplace at the far end and an equally large table ran the length of the room with benches on either side. Two smaller rooms were located behind the fireplace, accessed by a door on either side of the fireplace. A thick coat of dust covered the whole interior. Cobwebs hung from the roughhewn rafters, dust and dirt covered everything and it smelled of mold and mildew. Under her feet, Hannah felt large flat stones beneath the dirt as she approached the table.

"Welcome to my family home, such as it is." William spoke as they stood there surveying the interior. "It will take a little cleaning, but it will shelter us from the elements."

"A little cleaning?" Sarah raised an eyebrow. "Men." She shook her head and took a deep breath. "There is no time to waste. We will need brooms, rags and hot water. The shutters must be opened on all the windows to let the light in." Sarah mumbled something about her mother and she marched outside.

William smiled at Gavin and they both looked to Hannah who had no idea where to start or what to do so she followed Sarah through the door.

Once outside, Hannah paused to watch the men of the ship offloading supplies. The supplies began to form a small mountain between the quay and the long house. Crates and barrels were amassing faster that Hannah thought was possible.

"Gavin, stay with Sarah and Hannah. Do whatever they ask of you. I must get the horses ashore." William headed to the waterside.

"Milady Hannah, I would like to introduce you to my wife Betsy." Rory approached.

Betsy was a short woman, as big around as she was tall. Her fire, red hair tied back and reached the middle of her back in tight curls. Her cheeks were as red as her hair and her smile was huge. She wore a simple blue woolen kirtle over her bodice.

"Milady." Betsy bowed her head.

"I am most happy to meet you Betsy." Hannah took her hand. "And this is my maid, Sarah."

Sarah stepped forward and knelt. "Mistress Betsy."

"It is good to meet both of you as well. Rory says that you will be staying at the long house for a time. If I may be of any help, just let me know." Betsy eyes raked over them both over from head to toe.

Remembering she was still in boys clothing, Hannah started to explain. "You must be wondering—"

"My Rory has told me why you are here. You are safe. No harm will come to the daughter of Milord Edward."

"Thank you," Hannah, replied even though she did not fully understand Betsy's meaning.

"I must get back to the bairns. I see Rory has already slipped away to help Liam. He has been gone for more than six months and he thought he could distract me so I would not notice his escape. Men folk, when will they learn we can see right through them?" Betsy shook her head. "On the other hand, there is much to do now that Liam has returned." She watched the activity at the water's edge, walked away, and called back over her shoulder, "Don't worry about cooking, I have enough for everyone." She winked at the two women and left.

There was something most familiar about Rory's wife. The thought left her as they turned away.

Returning to the long house, Sarah covered their hair with a rag to protect it from the dirt. Hannah did likewise even though she had no idea where to begin so she followed her maid's lead, sweeping down cobwebs and knocking dirt from the walls. The air in the long house filled with dust motes as they swept the flagstone floor. Gavin was of great help providing them with hot water, soap, and cleaning supplies he had collected from Betsy. The two women scrubbed the long table, benches, and chairs with stiff brushes until their arms ached, and fingers wrinkled.

Under Sarah's directions, Gavin had the chore of climbing inside the chimney to dislodge bird's nests and other debris. Clouds of soot and ash fell. Having reached as high inside as he could go, Gavin stood inside the great stone fireplace covered head to toe in black and dirt. Hannah giggled at the sight of him. Sarah joined in and the three of them laughed until they cried. With her laughter under control, Hannah handed Gavin a bar of soap and sent him to away to wash. Hannah turned and went to work on the chains and hooks for suspending pots in the fireplace.

The day wore on, by mid-afternoon, Sarah stood with her hands on her hips, looking all around her with satisfaction on her face.

"Hannah, we have done well. I think we should clean the larder next. If the shelves in there are not covered with dead vermin, Gavin can get most of the provisions moved inside before dark."

"I have to admit, when I first saw the inside of this, I did not think anyone would ever be able to live here. Sarah, you are a harsh taskmaster. This room is... nice." She sat heavily on the end of a bench.

"Hannah I am sorry. I forgot that you are not used to this sort of... challenge."

"God's teeth, it is not like I have a full staff of servants to take over the tasks that must be completed."

The maid bit her bottom lip; nodding she said nothing.

Hannah got to her feet. "Well that larder room is not going to clean itself."

Much later stepping out of the larder, her task accomplished, Hannah found Gavin holding a large basket.

"Miss Betsy sent you these herbs for the floor and smaller bundled ones for the larder, she said they are fresh and need to be dried."

She reached for the small bundles, tied with care, one by one inhaling their aroma. "Sage, rosemary, thyme and lavender, this is wonderful!"

Gavin made a dash for the door leaving the women to stare at each other in his wake. Moments later he returned weighted down by the small keg. "She also sent this ale. She thought you might have worked up a thirst."

"All of this is very kind of her Gavin. But we have nothing to drink the ale from." Hannah glanced about the room.

Again, he rushed out. Sarah smiled after him. "That boy is so eager to please." She paused puzzlement crossed her face. "I wonder where his parents are."

"William has never mentioned Gavin's parents." Hannah frowned. "I will have to ask him about that. Along with a host of other questions."

Gavin ran back into the room, his arms loaded with pewter tankards.

"Gavin, pour for Mistress Hannah while I hang these in the larder," Sarah gathered the herb bundles.

"Yes ma'am." He went to work on the bung.

Left standing with nothing to do Hannah took up the basket by the handle and began strewing the aromatic rushes mixed with dried flowers and herbs on the floor. Their sweet clean scent floated on the air; pride filled her, pushing her fatigue back into the recesses of her mind. For the first time in her life, she had worked the majority of a day. She smiled and walked about the room. The bare wood walls and rafters were free of cobwebs, the table and benches were free of dirt. The stones around the fireplace and mantle no longer black with soot. While she had been cleaning in the larder Gavin had kept busy providing a stack of dried peat blocks near the fireplace and a small fire crackled providing a sense of welcome. The scent of peat smoke wafted through the room mixing with aroma of the herbs. Here there was no one to pamper her or bring her the things she requested. No house staff to see to all the daily chores. There was only herself, a maid, and a boy.

Now I am learning what being a woman is all about, Hannah mused.

This was hard work and I pulled my weight.

Through the window, she could see the setting sun peeping through the leaves on the trees above the quiet cove. Deep purple, orange and pink blended in the sky above the treetops. Yet another first in her life, Hannah paused to appreciate a sunset. It was as stunning as the one William had shared with her.

"I could use one of those." William's long strides carried him across the room where he downed a tankard, and handed it back to Gavin for a refill.

Hannah had been so absorbed in thought she had not heard him enter the house. She viewed him from head to toe. His hair slicked back, wet tied at the nape of his neck. He had on clean clothes and smelled of scented soap. Her head snapped down, she was dusty, dirty and gritty. There were sweat stains at her armpits and she smelled pungent. Her attempt to brush the grime away with her hands was useless.

William laughed, "Why, Hannah, I do believe this is the first time I have seen you so unkempt"

"We have been rather busy cleaning your home today." Her anger rising.

William looked about the house. "And, I must say, you have done a fine job. Well done, Hannah, well done." He extended his hand to her. "Betsy has sent me to fetch you and Sarah. Rory killed a deer this day and it has been roasting on the spit for hours. She asks that all of us to join her and her family down by the fire pit for an evening meal."

Shaking her head, "I must wash first. I cannot go like this." She ran to a bucket of water left over from cleaning. Splashed water over her face and hair, and dried her face on the rag from her hair. Using one of the stiff cleaning brushes, she brushed most of the dirt off her breeches. She ran into the sleeping room, changed into a clean shirt, remembering the comfort of a hot bath.

Hannah walked beside William, Gavin and Sarah close behind, to the yard and across to the fire pit. Rory and his family were sitting to one side of the pit away from the smoke as they arrived. Betsy filled wooden trenchers one by one and handed them out. Her oldest son filled tankards of ale and then sat beside his father. Everyone sat on the ground forming a circle around the fire to eat their evening meal of fresh venison, warm bread and boiled greens.

Rory and William discussed the ship sailing on the morning tide.

Betsy and Sarah talked about the provisions on the quay waiting to be unpacked and delivered to the storehouse. Gavin visited with Rory's boys, talking of things that interest all boys of any age; they giggled and laughed as they ate. Quietly beside William, Hannah ate her meal in silence, listening to the conversations around her. Her arms, shoulders and neck ached. Never could she remember being so hungry and tired. The smell of the wood smoke mingled with the aroma of the deer meat on the spit. Before she realized, her trencher was empty and she sat back cradling her tankard in her lap stifling a yawn.

"How long will you be staying William?" Betsy leaned forward.

"I do not know. There are too many factors, a month, six months, maybe more." William shrugged his shoulders. "Edward indicated that he would come to us. We will remain here until he arrives."

"The clan will have heard by now of your return. They will want to see you." Rory kicked at the fire with his toe.

"Aye, there is that." William emptied his tankard and sat it down. "They will want news from England. Some will want to return now the burnings have stopped."

"That will be their decision and their choice. I do not understand why anyone would want to leave Ireland." Betsy looked at her husband. "This is where I have lived my whole life and this is where I will raise our bairns. This is home."

"Some folks have different ideas about life Betsy." Rory placed his arm around her.

"Aye and you are one of them." She pushed him away playfully.

"Some folk just accept where they are and make the most of it." Hannah spoke, her head resting on William's arm. "Sarah, it is time for us to retire for the night."

Looking down at her, William nodded. "I think a hard day's work agreed with you."

She swallowed a sharp retort, forced a weak smile. "Good night."

William stood and helped her to her feet. Hannah marched away without a word. Once in the bedroom she pulled off her breeches and shirt, slipped into a shift and slipped between the covers. Sarah prepared a pallet on the floor, pulled the wool blanket up to her chin, and fell asleep.

Watching Hannah walk away, William was lost in his own thoughts. She had been through so much. A brutal rape, beaten and now learning to survive in a world that she was not accustomed to. Amazed by her adaptability of being out of her element, he marveled at her jumping in to ready the hall instead of complaining and leaving all the work to Sarah and Gavin. She was stronger than she knew, and she was not aware of it. The thought of drawing her into her father's web of spies gave him doubt. However, it was too late to second guess the choice. The education Edward had given her had more than one purpose and the need was great. Deciphering codes would keep her busy and give him the freedom to further their goals. At least she was safe here. Edward's legacy would live on through her.

"Good night Hannah," he whispered. "Perhaps one day..." He left the thought unfinished and walked into the night.

The next morning Hannah awoke sore and stiff. With no idea what the day would bring and determined to keep up with Sarah, she pushed Freya off her and dressed in clean breeches and shirt. Freya was here! She barely remembered Gavin bringing the cat to her during the night. He had the cat held firmly in his arms, calling her name just above a whisper until she had opened her eyes. Still half asleep, she remembered thanking him and curling the cat close to her stomach. She had gone promptly back to sleep.

Looking about the house, she was alone except for the cat. Freya's green eyes absorbed everything about the large room. She stretched and pawed playfully at the rushes on the floor. Hannah watched her for a moment, wondered where everyone was, she left the house. Looking across the harbor, she took a deep breath of the fresh sea air. There were voices coming from behind the long house. She followed the noise and found Sarah surrounded by a small group of women. A small girl tugged on the sleeve of Sarah's shirt and looked at Hannah. Sarah excused herself and met Hannah a short distance away.

"Come join us," she slipped her arm around Hannah's waist. "They started arriving soon after day break. They heard William had returned. There are more people arriving by the hour. Repairs are virtually completed; a garden is being planted and the majority of women are cooking down by the pit. The harbor and quay are being made ready for ships. Even the horses have a new home!" Excitement showed in Sarah's voice as she escorted Hannah to the other women.

"Where did they all come from?" Hannah whispered.

"Everywhere, or at least from all around here." Sarah smiled and then turned to the women who had become quiet.

"Ladies, this is Milord Edward's daughter, Mistress Hannah." Sarah laughed and then whispered in Hannah's ear, "I have met so many I cannot remember everyone's name."

Suddenly Hannah was surrounded by a sea of female faces. A cacophony of voices all speaking to her at the same time was overwhelming. Hannah smiled and nodded to each one in turn. Their numbers grew, as she turned first this way then that way and back again. So many unwashed bodies, the smell assaulted her nose. She tried to back away but found her path hampered by even more women. Panic began to build in her chest; her breath was coming faster and faster.

Ready to bolt, Hannah froze; a loud popping sound came from her right. Her head snapped around. A short, overweight, red haired woman approached clapping her hands. "Enough, lazing around. There are hardworking people to feed. To work with all of you."

A wave of quiet spread through the mass of women, they dropped their heads and turned away. This new arrival stood with her hands on her broad hips scowling at them. Her hair cut short in an unbecoming fashion. She wore a sturdy dark grey woolen gown with a black skirt. Her face broke into an insincere smile as their eyes met.

She proceeded to send the women scurrying in all directions by shouting. "The long house needs a good cleaning now that her highness is awake. Barrels and crates to unpack. And more food to be prepared for all these hungry mouths, there is more coming I am sure. I want to know how you expect all of this to get done while you stand around like a gaggle of stupid geese."

One of the younger women leaned in close to Hannah. "That's Margaret. She thinks she is in charge of everything - very bossy." She rolled her eyes. "She scares me." She bowed her head and disappeared.

Hannah took a deep breath, ignoring Margaret, and looked to the activity going on around her. Men, of all shapes and sizes, were putting the final changes to a horse stable, roofs in the process of being repaired. Huge stones were being moved at the quay. A multitude of women were preparing food or adding wood and peat to the fire pit. Children of all ages were scattered everywhere. Some were preparing food, while others had the task of cooking. Laughing, cries, and conversations assaulted her ears.

Large clouds of dust emitted from all the buildings, as they were cleaned. All of the buildings, except Betsy's. Unable to locate Betsy,

Hannah searched the crowds for Sarah and could not find her either.

A loud clearing of the throat drew Hannah's attention back to Margaret, who stood a few feet away studying Hannah. "Are you going to stand there all day, or are you going to go to work?" Margaret demanded.

"Perhaps you do not know to whom you speak," Hannah responded, her pulse quickened and her eyes flashed. "How dare you speak to me in this manner?"

Margaret raised her eyebrows. "I don't care if you are the Queen of England herself. There is work to be done."

Hannah opened her mouth to speak.

"Here you are, Hannah. I have been looking everywhere for you." William smiled down at her. He took her by the elbow, he said "Margaret, excuse us. I have business to discuss with Mistress Hannah."

"Oh." Margaret appeared to be contrite.

Walking away, Hannah worked on controlling her anger. "Who is that most foul woman?"

William chuckled. "That is Margaret O'Brady. And yes, she can be most foul."

"Why?"

"I suppose it is because she is very angry and lonely. Her husband set sail from this very quay and never returned." William explained leading her alongside the quay.

"Oh. So, he died at sea." Hannah was beginning to feel sympathy for Margaret.

William laughed. "O'Brady is alive and well. Margaret knows he lives on the other side of Ireland with another woman and their five children. I think it was about four years ago, Margaret finally took up with another man after her husband refused to return having become a devout Catholic. Margaret became angrier than usual and the new man, well, he left her as well."

Hannah listened to the scandal. "Sounds like she is a very unhappy woman and wants everyone around her to be just as unhappy." She looked up at William, "Is that why you rescued me from her?"

"Yes and no." William glanced around them before he spoke again. "Charles found a packet hidden in with the cargo on the ship. He sent it to me before he set sail. It is from an informant in France to another in Spain. I think both are employed by the Spanish crown. I attempted to translate some of the contents but, my Spanish is not what it should be. Would you translate and copy them tonight in private?"

"I will try. Who will the copy be sent to?"

"Your father."

Hannah nodded, her chest tightened at the thought of her father. She wondered how long before he arrived and when she could go home. They were quiet as they walked back into the throng of activity. People smiled, waved and greeted William as they passed. Hannah puzzled over the appearance of all the strangers that were everywhere today. "William, where did all these people come from? And why?"

"They have come from their homes all over this part of county Wexford, because Liam Mac Murchadha has returned. When my father died, I became the head of the clan, a relatively small clan but, a clan none the less. Once the work is completed there will be a grand celebration." William explained, he led her back to the long house.

"I have known you my whole life. Yet, I have learned more about you in the past month than all the years combined. But I am still confused," Hannah stopped. "In England you are William O'Murphy and here Liam Mac Murchadha."

"Our family name is Mac Murchadha of the clan Mac Murchadha. William O'Murphy is the English version."

"What does Mac Murchadha mean?"

"Simply put, it means Sea Warrior."

"How fitting." She smiled looking out across the harbor. "What are those men doing over there?"

"They are setting the cannon into place. There are two on the peninsula, one points out to sea and the other aimed just before the entrance to the harbor. Here on the quay side," he pointed further down, "there are two more, one aimed at the entrance, the other aimed straight across. See the large standing stones on either side of the entrance?"

"Yes."

"The chain from the cargo hold has been anchored to the other side. On this side, it is attached to a harness. In the event an unfriendly ship makes its way through the cannon fire, it can be stopped by pulling the chain up from the floor of the harbor. It only has to be close to the surface to stop a ship. It will work preventing one from leaving, should the need arise."

"You expect trouble?" Hannah shielded her eyes from the sun and surveyed everything he had explained.

"We are preparing. If one is not prepared, one will not survive. That is the way of life. I wish to grow old and watch my future children grow into adulthood."

"I think I understand. But there is one thing I do not understand. Everyone has come here to get a job done. They have something to accomplish, something to do. What should I be doing?" She looked in his eyes with earnest.

"You are to be yourself." His smile was genuine it spread throughout his face. "Inside I have a surprise. Sarah is expecting you and will explain everything."

Opening the door to the long house, he bowed over her hand, his lips touching briefly. "Until tonight milady," he turned and walked away.

Mystified by his actions she touched her hand where his lips had lightly touched, a shiver ran through her. She was shocked by her own reaction. Deep inside, she felt different. Upon waking, she had been determined to whatever the day required of her. Her encounter with Margaret had made her angry. Now, William had left her with a new emotion. She was happy. She had no right to feel happy here, this was not her home. These were not her people. The reason she was here was due to the vile things Thomas had done to her, followed by her killing him. He had destroyed her sense of belonging. She was here in Ireland because she of a warrant for murder. A murder she had committed after being beaten and raped by her beloved husband. That had been two months ago, a lifetime ago. Not only had her life changed, her sense of direction was changed forever.

She froze with fear.

Chapter Twenty-Four

Hannah stood unmoving in the main room of the long house. Windows and the door were shut. Flames in the fireplace licked and consumed the peat bricks sending the welcoming aroma throughout the space. Her mind was racing.

Two months. She had not had her courses in two months, not since before the wedding. No. No, she could not be with child. This was not how it was to be. A child should be conceived in love. Fear grew in the pit of her stomach her breath became rapid. Beads of cold sweat broke out all over her body. She felt faint, and stepped into the long house. She did not want to have a child that would be a constant reminder of Thomas' cankered heart.

Halfway across the floor she stopped. Moments passed before her eyes adjusted. The long tables and benches had been removed. She could smell the peat smoke from the fire burning in the fireplace under an iron pot the hung up high above the flames.

"Hannah, is that you?" Sarah's voice drifted from the sleeping room. "I am here."

Sarah popped her head around the corner. "Come see…" Sarah rushed forward. "Oh my, are you ill? You are as pale as milk."

"I am…" Hannah tried to focus on Sarah.

Taking Hannah by the arm, "I asked too much of you yesterday. You are not used to such things." She led her to the sleeping room, and eased Hannah onto the large over stuffed bed. "Sit here while I get you something to eat and drink." She turned and left.

Okay, Hannah, breathe remain calm. Breathe. Sarah must not know. No one must know. Just breathe. Hannah closed her eyes and breathed, long, deep breaths, forcing thoughts to calm. Moments ago, she was happy, all the horror forgotten.

If terrible events could come rushing in on her then she could force them away. *Breathe and lock them away until I can be alone with them. Then*

I will sort out what to do, and not let memories over power. I will maintain Sarah's notion of my not used to working. It was believable. I will not allow Thomas to continue to ruin my life. He is dead and I have survived. I shall continue to survive and rise above all of this. Forcing her mind blank, she straightened her shoulders with determination.

Sarah returned carrying a wooden tray two tankards teetered on a tray. The smell of boiled cabbage and meat filled the room. She sat on the bed with the tray resting between them.

"Here, drink," she said as she handed Hannah a tankard of ale. "Eat, you will feel better with a full stomach."

Hannah forced a smile and downed the ale. Sarah's words from moments ago came to her. "There was something you wanted me to see?"

"Yes," she motioned to two new trunks against the far wall. "William brought you a new gown to wear tonight. I have water heating for bathing before you try it on. If needs be, there is time enough for any alterations."

"What gown and what is so special about tonight?" Hannah tried to focus on Sarah's words, reaching for the other tankard.

"Eat and I will explain." Excitement filled her voice.

The smell of the cabbage turned Hannah's stomach and she pushed the tray away.

"Captain Charles discovered a trunk with the cargo from the ship we were on. The trunk contained two gowns intended for Spain. William had them delivered here for us to wear tonight. I have never seen anything so exquisite." She flew across the room to the largest trunk in the corner. She picked up a mass of red linen, turning, she held it in front of her so Hannah could see the gown. Cream-colored flowers and leaves wove their way through the fabric enhanced by thread of gold that reflected the light streaming into the room's single window. A square neckline with attached sleeves, both were trimmed with cream-colored lace.

Hannah rose and reached for the gown, her fingers caressed the fabric. "Sarah, this was intended for royalty. I cannot wear this." Shaking her head, she backed away from the gown.

"Master William said you would say that. He also said that not wearing this gown is not an option. He insists." Sarah laid the gown on the bed with great care and removed the tray to the windowsill. "He said his return is a great event and that you are the only person of standing to be at his side as hostess. You cannot appear dressed as a boy. He also said that this is a great honor to you and your father."

"I cannot deny I desire to wear something so grand." Hannah's hand lay upon the gown as she sat down beside it. Her eyes fixed on the superb cloth and fine sewing. Tearing her gaze away, she looked to Sarah. "You said there were two such gowns?"

Sarah beamed. "Yes, the other is modest." She retrieved the second from the trunk. She held a solid cream-colored gown up to her body. "William said I am to wear this one."

"William insisted?" Hannah looked back to the red cloth spilling across the bed.

"Yes ma'am."

"Very well, for William." Hannah agreed with a twinge of guilt for the lady who would never receive the royal gown.

"There is something else I must tell you." Sarah put the gown she held back into the trunk. Kneeling beside to the smaller trunk that held her and Hannah's everyday clothes, she rummaged through and pulled out a small, folded, brown piece of cloth.

Facing Hannah, she explained. "I have kept this a secret from you. Forgive me. I did not know when to return this. But now seems like the right time." Sarah laid the cloth in Hannah's lap.

The cloth was heavier than it should be. With curious reluctance, she unfolded it. Her hands began to tremble and tears filled her eyes as she saw the necklace her father had given her on her wedding day. "This was my mother's. I thought beyond hope of ever seeing it again. Thank you."

Hannah clutched the necklace to the heart. Tears fell down her cheeks.

"There is more." With trepidation, Sarah placed something cold, hard and heavy in Hannah's hand. "I did not know what to do with this. I took it off your finger the night we escaped."

Hannah looked at the gold ring in the palm of her hand, her wedding ring. Pain gripped her heart as she stared. Unwanted memories filled her. *Control, I must maintain control.*

She looked around the rustic room with the open glassless window. Fresh air filled her lungs as she inhaled in the attempt to remain calm. She sat upon the bed with soft woolen blankets. A wooden plank door hung in the doorway in the rock wall that held the fireplace on the other side. Other furniture in the room included a simple but sturdy table with three stools, a couple of shelves on the other wall, three trunks of various sizes and a small crate of books. Simple furnishings for a simple way of life.

"I would rather spend the rest of my days here in this rustic room than spend one minute with the monster I married." Her voice composed. Her face showed no emotion. She handed Sarah the ring. "Put this away. I never want to see it again. Perhaps, one day I will sell it. For I know not what shall become of me. All prospects of my making a good marriage have fled." Unthinking, her hand went to her stomach.

Closing her hand around the ring, Sarah turned away.

"Bring water, I would like to wash my hair and bathe for tonight." Hannah released her grip on the silver emerald necklace, a bead of blood appeared in her palm. In her effort to remain in control, she had forgotten the precious jewels of her mother.

***

Twilight descended on Ireland, Hannah stood just outside the long house door. Tables with benches had been set up in the yard. One appeared to sit higher than the others, facing the fire pit. Two young men stood at the pit turning a large beast over the flames. The smell of roasting meat mingled with brine, hung in the air. People, dressed their best created a rainbow of color, milled around in conversation; the sound of laughter filled the air. Sons and daughters carried pots and trenchers from the pit to the surrounding tables under the direction of their elders.

"Milady, you are most beautiful." William stepped in front of Hannah and bowed. "May I escort you to your seat?" He held out his hand for her.

"You may milord," Hannah tilted her head forward, placing her hand in his.

William burst into laughter. All heads turned, he led her by the hand to the raised table. William stood at the table with Hannah. All eyes fell on them as quiet descended on the crowd. Hannah stood erect with her chin held firm. The fire reflected off the gold thread of her gown and the silver and emerald necklace at her throat.

"This must be how Queen Elizabeth feels every time she dines at court," Hannah whispered.

Raising his tankard, William addressed the crowd, "Clan Mac Murchadha, welcome!" A roar of cheers rose from the throng of people. Taking his place beside her, he motioned for the feast to begin.

The people marched from table to table with mountains of food on trenchers. Before Hannah, the table laden with roasted boar, venison, fowl, and fish. Dishes of berries and nuts along with fresh baked bread and golden honey. Simple foods prepared with love and skill by the women present. Everyone ate their fill as the tankards were refilled repeatedly.

Forcing a smile, on the inside panic gripped Hannah. Pushing her food about the trencher and taking a small bite now and then, she focused on controlling the nausea that clawed at her stomach. The odor of so many bodies pressed together, the food, smoke from the pit and the sudden lack of a breeze, weakened her resolve. She plucked a mint leaf from a nearby dish, folded bread around the herb and chewed it slow and cautious.

The feeding frenzy slowed, a man with a grey beard stood and raised his tankard. "Liam, welcome home."

His words were drowned out by another roar of cheers. A chant rose among the men "Liam, Liam, Liam." One by one every man present stood to welcome William home and to swear his fealty.

Standing, William praised each man for deeds accomplished during the years of his absence. One had kept Betsy and her children in fresh meat and game. Another had organized a group of men to dig a well for a neighbor. Yet another man had saved a family's milk cow from certain death, after the cow had become stuck in mud after heavy rains. The list continued until everyone had received praise from William.

William held his tankard above his head, "Let us all drink to the continuing health, prosperity and strength of our Clan, Ireland, and Queen Elizabeth and England."

All present raised their tankards and began to chant "Liam". Their voices raised and grew louder and louder, until at last someone yelled above the din "Music! Let there be music!" On cue, tables and benches were carried farther away from the fire pit. A small group of men assembled to one side placing stools in a small cluster. Within moments, they took their places and began tuning their lutes, harps and a bodhrán. The music was lively, and a circle formed around the pit, everyone was anxious to begin the first dance of the evening.

Overseeing the festivities, William sat at the center of the raised table. Hannah watched the dancing and William at the same time. She marveled how he had taken the time to think of her lack of apparel during his day's activities. He had never been married as far as she knew. What was there in him to think beyond his usual scope of undertakings and remember she was still in breeches? Is this the way of a man? Yes, Father had provided for her clothing, but that was what a father was supposed to do. Perhaps William was following Father's orders to provide for her. Maybe it was Charles's idea to be rid of the feminine cargo before sailing.

Was it proper for her to have accepted the gown? What would people think? What would they say? She was a defiled woman accepting gifts of a personal nature from a man not her father or her husband. Squirming in her seat she pushed the idea away.

A young man approached Sarah as she sat smiling and humming with the music. He appeared to be several years younger than Sarah. His red hair combed back and tied at the nape of his neck. He wore a simple tunic and matching brown breeches. He smiled at Sarah, bowed formally, and offered her his hand in invitation to join the dancing. Sarah beamed at him and then turned to Hannah asking permission.

Granting permission with a nod of her head, she watched Sarah bow to the man. He took her hand and they ran to join the circle.

"Ireland is agreeing with her, she looks happy." William leaned closer to be heard over the clamor.

"She was most happy earlier today when she revealed the gowns you had provided for us." Hannah turned so her words could be heard. "I have not had the opportunity to thank you for them. They are truly beautiful. Thank you."

"Gowns and such are an added bonus, information is foremost important. But, you are welcome." He then changed the subject. "Seeing Sarah have fun for a change does my heart good. With everything the two of you have been through." He turned to face her. "She refused to leave you when I made plans to send her back to England. That is true loyalty."

"She stayed for me?" There was a tug at Hannah's heart.

"She was most adamant, to the peak of being insubordinate. Now, as an afterthought, I am grateful to her for being so. I don't think we could have pulled off our little ruse without her."

"She has been a sister to me. I have never told her how much she means to me. Not once." Sadness filled Hannah, how could she be so thoughtless.

"You will have plenty of time to tell her. But for now…" William stood, bowed and held out his hand for Hannah. "Milady, will you dance with me?"

"I do not know the steps."

"That I shall remedy." He took her hand, pulling her to her feet.

They joined the circle with William on her left. He leaned his head to her. "First take six quick steps to your left, and then the same to the right." Hannah followed his instructions. "Now we let go our hands and face each other, holding up our right arms. One step to the left, one to the right, another to the right and now turn to the left. Circle around and stop where you began. Well done!" He smiled down at her.

Following his lead, she concentrated on his words. Feeling herself once again. The faces around her were but a blur as she forgot the recent past. They danced through the smoke of the pit and she found herself laughing along with the crowd.

"Is Irish dancing so different from English?" He laughed.

"Not at all." Smiling up at him, she held on to his hand.

"Now step to the left, raise your left heel and slide your right foot to the left and lower your heel." Laughing together, he continued, "Step to the left, kick with the right and hop. Step to the left and slide the right and hop." The music faded. William turned her to face him. "And now, an honor, we do this together." He slid his right foot back, bent his right knee, bowing to her as she bowed to him.

Hannah's cheeks were flushed as she bowed to him a second time. An excellent dancer, William proved to be superb at teaching as well. Another thing she had not known about him. Her father had personally seen to her education. In itself this was not uncommon when no male heir was forth coming. It is expected of royalty. There was so much more to learn. Over the past few weeks William had continued her education in ways she never thought of. Here she was learning Irish dance, and she wanted more. More of the world around her. Nothing would hold her back, nothing except being tarnished, pregnant and wanted for murder.

The dancing continued and Hannah looked at the faces around her. The clan O'Murphy was celebrating for the first time in years. All thoughts of daily survival, labor, and the changes of the world were far from their minds tonight. Tonight was for joyous celebration. The Irish were known for celebrating as hard as they toiled. Hannah admired how exuberant the clan was. There was no class separation. These people were boisterous, energetic and carefree and she was one of them. If only for the moment.

The dance ended, William pulled Hannah aside, almost out of breath. "I am an old man Hannah. I must take a break. Will you join me for a pint?"

Just as breathless Hannah beamed up at him, her cheeks flushed and the shimmer of sweat glistened in the fire light. "Yes, I would like that very much!"

He left her and returned with two flagons of ale. "We may find a cool breeze quay side."

They walked side by side to the quay. A few feet before the water's edge they came to a large flat stone. William removed his doublet and spread it across the stone for Hannah to sit. "Please share a seat with me, there is ample room." He took her hand until she was seated.

Hannah drank deeply from the pewter flagon. Behind them, there was a pause in the music. Ever so soft, a sound could be heard. She turned her head trying to locate the source. The volume was increasing bit by bit. Music, unlike any she had heard before. The music grew louder; the tune touched every part of her being. Still she could not find the source or the location from which it came. "William? What is it I hear?"

"Irish pipes. They are playing a tribute to the members of clan Mac Murchadha that are no longer with us. It is a tradition that goes back as far as I can remember. No one knows who is playing and they play unseen, so the tradition goes. Later tonight several sets of pipes will join the other musicians and the dancing will continue till dawn." He drank from his flagon.

"The sound is magnificent." Hannah closed her eyes and let the music wash over her. She could feel each note touching deep inside her. Her soul was at peace. The final note enveloped her in its arms, caressing her. The single note held on. Just when Hannah thought it would last forever, the sound began to fade. Then there was silence. Hannah opened her eyes. She felt as if her entire body was on edge, there was a yearning deep inside of her.

Her senses were awakened. The ale tasted sweeter, the air smelled cleaner, the breeze cooler, and she could hear the gentle lapping of the water along with the sounds of the people behind her back. They spoke in hushed tones as one does in church.

William sat, inches away from her. She could feel the heat of his body radiating. The breeze carried the scent of his sweat mingled with the salty air. She was aware of how close he was. Her heart quickened as though they were still dancing. She looked around, looking for anything that would take her mind away from the thought of him.

The breezed cooled her face as it continued on to cause the slightest ripple on top of the water of the harbor. A full moon reflected upon seawater. The moon's brightness mirroring the one that was hanging above the tree tops on the hill across from where they sat. Shades of black faded and mixed with shades of blue. The light from the two moons shined as beacons form the gods. The beauty of this place filled her soul, as England never could. England… home… was her father looking on the same moon and thinking of her?

"William, do you know when my father shall come?"

"No. I know no more than you do. He said he would come to you. So we must wait." He looked across the harbor. "While we wait, we will gather as much information as comes our way to give to him. I think he will not come as soon as you would like. He too must be careful, in case he is watched and followed. He would not want to lead Phillip to you. Your safety is foremost on his mind."

"I have made such a mess of things." Hannah lowered her head. "Had I waited for Thomas to come to me instead of searching him out none of this would have happened. The blame rests with me."

"No!" William jumped to his feet. "Your father knew Thomas was not as he seemed. By now, he knows what he was about. Everything that transpired is Thomas' fault, not yours!" His face hidden by shadow. The moon light revealed only his silhouette.

"I was the one who fell in love with him. I wanted to wed him."

"You wed a spoilt boy, next time try a man." His voice was cold and hard as he extended his hand. Hannah took his hand and stood. She could feel his anger and could see it in the way he squared his shoulders as William retrieved his doublet. They walked back to the gathering without speaking. Not knowing who he was angry with, she worried her lip with her teeth. All she knew was that the joy of the evening had left the two of them.

"Liam. Liam." The frantic voice came from a figure running from the far side of the harbor. Quiet fell upon the gathering as everyone turned. Out of breath, a boy ran into the light of the fire. "Liam, a ship is coming. With no signal, it is rounding the point." He stopped, bent over his knees trying to catch his breath.

William was on alert. "Rory, man the chain and the cannon. Prepare for attack!" He ordered. "Betsy, take care of the women!" He shouted over his shoulder, and he disappeared into the darkness.

Chapter Twenty-Five

Everyone moved as one. Water doused the fire. Steam rose in a single column above the hissing fire as it died. The torches extinguished. Children ran to gather food and carry it away while the women began lifting tables and benches. Everything returned to its proper place with the precision of a military encampment. Hannah and Sarah joined in moving quickly as Betsy called out directions. Once the area was cleared, Betsy called out "Arm your selves."

Women scattered and then regrouped, headed for the long house. Women and children alike held knives, hatchets, rakes, and walking sticks. A few had swords at their sides. Betsy appeared with a cross bow in hand, a quiver over her shoulder.

Once inside the shutters and the door was secured. A hush fell over the long house as everyone strained to hear any sound that might tell what was transpiring at the harbor. The smell of fear and the press of unwashed bodies caused bile to rise in Hannah's throat. The rushes and herbs being crushed under so many feet were no match for the stench that assaulted Hannah's nose. She pushed her way through the sea of women to the ash bucket by the fireplace and vomited. Sarah was at her side as she straightened.

"We are safe here. William will see to it." Sarah assured her.

Hannah nodded and bent to vomit again.

Down through the ages, women have waited for word from their men at battle, just as these women did tonight. They wondered if they would ever see their husbands, brothers, and sons alive again. They prepared themselves mentally for the possibility of having already had that last dance, last word or that last embrace. They braced themselves and waited. Understanding this, Hannah watched them, minutes passed. A baby began to cry, a mother could be heard whispering in Irish to quiet the child's fear. Small children sat on the floor, their backs against the wall. Women and the older girls shifted and formed clusters throughout the room. More time passed and still no word reached them. Some whispered in quiet conversation while others whispered prayers. Hannah held her cutlass, and could feel the knife against her thigh tucked inside her nether stocking. They gave her comfort though she could feel her courage waning as time passed.

Sarah indicated with a nod. Hannah looked in the direction of Sarah's gaze. Betsy stood blocking the doorway overlooking the room and its contents. She stood as firm and solid as the door itself. Hannah turned back to Sarah and together they both stood a little straighter. Whatever transpired this night, they were not alone; they would all face it together.

A knock sounded on the door. Everyone startled. Those sitting jumped to their feet. All heads turned to the door. "All is well. Open the door." William's voice carried through the door. "We have wounded."

The door swung open and the women began filing out. Sarah and Hannah opened the shutters as they reached them on their way to the door. Betsy stopped them before they could exit. "Go to the larder and find as many bolts of cotton as you can. Tear it into strips for bandages. I will be right back." She disappeared into the night.

Hannah was lighting candles when Rory carried in the first wounded sailor and laid him on the table. Sarah came running out of the larder with a bolt of pale green cotton in her arms. She threw it on the end of the table and rushed to Rory, looking down at the sailor she asked, "What has happened?"

"They were fired upon by a Spanish ship. This here, is the first mate, their captain is missing. They were the only two that knew the signal for our harbor. The ship is listing and we do not know how many survived or how many are wounded." Rory turned and left.

Sarah led the way back across the room and lit a candle from the fireplace. "Light the others and I will get the cotton."

Sarah went back to the bolt of cloth and began to tear in into strips. Hannah continued lighting candles as her eyes fixed on the man lying unmoving on the table. Blood began to drip onto the floor. Hannah crossed the floor and handed Sarah the candle she carried. "Here take this and I will do the bandages."

Sarah took the candle and sat it in the center of the table. "Roll up the strips once you come to the end. That is how mother always did it."

Betsy came through the door carrying a large basket. Rory and

William were close behind. They supported a wounded man between them. Margaret O'Brady and two elderly women followed them. William and Rory laid the man on the table and made a hasty exit. Margaret stopped just inside the door with her hands on her hips surveying the scene before her. Her eyes jumped back and forth between Hannah and Sarah, she commanded them. "Ladies we are going to need water from the harbor. Both hot and cold will be necessary." She began to roll up her sleeves.

Betsy turned to her. "I thank you for offering to take care of that chore Margaret, because I need these two to assist me here." Betsy never looked up from the wounded men.

Margaret and her companions went to the larder and returned with their arms laden with buckets. Margaret glared at Betsy as she walked past headed for the door.

Once the three were out the door Betsy turned to Hannah, "I will not have her ordering you around in your own home."

"But this is William's home. I am a guest here." Hannah's voice was meek.

"You are Edward's daughter. As long as you are here, this is your home. Now, there is work to be done." Betsy looked at the unconscious men on the long table. "Miss Hannah, would you add more peat to the fire and then light as many candles as you can find." Betsy went to the first man she took a deep breath. "Sarah I need you to cut his clothes away so I can see how bad the wound is."

The women proceeded with their given tasks while more men with the wounded streamed into the room. Hannah became aware only the most seriously injured were brought into the long house. The other wounded sailors, who could make their own way off the ship, was heard, gathering in groups around a new fire that was blazing brightly in the pit.

Their voices carried on the slight breeze as they spoke in low tones. The flames from the fire could be seen through the doorway. Hannah watched them being served the remains of the feast and another barrel of ale had been brought up from the storehouse. People that had been celebrating were now caring for the wounded on the same spot they had danced only hours ago.

The last of the candles were burning brightly, Margaret and one of her companions carried buckets of water inside. They headed to the fireplace and filled the cauldron that Sarah used for heating water.

Margaret mumbled something under her breath as they left to join the others outside. Hannah remembered Betsy's words. She wondered about the reverence Betsy held regarding her father. Betsy spoke as if she knew Edward. But how? Father had never mentioned Ireland except in her geography lessons.

A cry from one of the men lying on the table brought Hannah's thoughts back to her the task. She watched as Sarah finished cutting the clothes off the first man, and moved on to the next. Hannah walked up beside Betsy awaiting instructions.

Betsy looked to her. "Hannah I need you to wash the wounds. When you finish with one, move on to the next as Sarah is doing. There are so many burns I cannot see what needs to be done." Hannah was horrified.

Patting her shoulder, "You'll be fine. I need to fetch some whiskey." She turned and walked away.

Taking a deep breath Hannah did everything asked of her. There were moments that she had to wait for Sarah to finish cutting clothes so she went back to making bandages.

Having returned, Betsy applied salves from her basket, removed foreign objects protruding through skin and all three assisted each other applying bandages. Stepping out to vomit on occasion, Hannah always returned to her post.

William joined them and worked side by side with Betsy. When necessary, he held one of the men down while Betsy extracted large shards of wood from the wound. Clansmen wandered in and out, removing men from the long table to blankets on the floor along the walls. They took away the ones who did not survive.

Still more wounded were carried in. Hannah continued, to step away from the table several times throughout the night to vomit. The smell of blood, bowels, burnt flesh and urine filled the room. The floor became slick with blood and human excrement. When she could stomach the gore no longer she made more bandages, and gave Betsy's tinctures to those lying on the floor when they begged, or their cries were more than she could deal with. It hurt her heart to see so many in such pain.

Stepping away from the table just long enough to show Hannah how to pulverize herbs with a mortar and pestle, Betsy also explained to her how to measure and mix them with honey or lard to form a paste as her supply dwindled. They were running out of everything except wounded men.

The night wore on, and the last of the wounded were attended to. Their screams and cries had quieted to moans and labored breathing. There was nothing left to do but wait. Hannah looked across the room at Sarah. Her cream-colored gown now stained red and brown with blood. Glancing down, the red gown she wore was ruined as well. Hannah stepped out of the long house. The predawn air was mercifully free of the pungent stench of blood. A cooling breeze touched her face and she welcomed the fresh air. Her shoulders drooped; she could not remember a time when she was this tired. Betsy sat on a bench near the rekindled fire that had been the center of joy the evening before. Hannah joined her, sitting heavy with the weight of the blood soaked gown and fatigue. She stared into the flames, her mind numb.

"You did well in there tonight, colleen." Betsy spoke without moving.

"Thank you." Hannah took a deep breath trying to get the stench of blood out of her nose. Moments passed as the two women sat, each lost in their own thoughts.

"I am with child." Hannah blurted out.

"I know. Do you wish to be rid of it?" Betsy's voice held no emotion.

"Yes." She answered as if in prayer.

"Come see me on the morrow, after you have rested." Betsy stood and walked into the night.

After a few hours of sleep, Hannah woke mid-morning. She pulled on a simple gown and wrapped a cloak across her shoulders. Bright sun light flooded the room through the open windows when she stepped into the long room. Sarah and four young women were tending to the needs of the wounded on the floor. Blankets were removed as the men who had occupied them walked away, or died during the night. Hannah did not know which. She knew she had seen enough of the results of battle to last her a lifetime. The smell of blood and gore still lingered in the room.

Sarah caught sight of her, "Good morrow."

"Good morrow." A good morrow for some she thought. Not so good for others. "I am off to see Betsy. She asked me to stop by after I had rested. I will return to help."

"Do you want me to accompany you?" Sarah was wiping her hands on her skirt.

"No. These men need you. I shall not be long."

Sarah turned back to the wounded man she had been tending. There was gentleness in her voice as she spoke to him. She held the wooden spoon with great care as she fed him.

I must speak to her soon and tell her everything. I must tell her how grateful I am for her. Hannah left the long house headed away from the harbor to the cottage Betsy and Rory called home. Some of the wounded still gathered about the pit. Margaret was changing the bandage of one of them that had a head wound. Their eyes met, Margaret glared at her.

Hannah raised her chin and continued. She could feel Margaret's eyes follow her. She had created an enemy and had no idea how or why. Perhaps Betsy could explain, or William.

William. So much had transpired last evening and through the night. She had not been able to take the time to process his sudden anger at the quay. His exact words were "You wed a spoiled boy, next time try a man." He had been angry, but why?

She had made a huge mistake. She had taken responsibility for the error and voiced that to him. Was he angry because Thomas's death had caused a change in his plans with her father? Did he consider her a burden and wish for father to come soon so he would no longer be responsible for her? The thought of him being angry with her did not sit well. She wanted Williams's approval and support. But why was his approval important to her?

She was ashamed. A raging sea of shame washed over her. She was no longer the person she had been raised to be. Nor was she the woman she aspired to become. Married a sodomite, committed murder, widowed and pregnant, and wanted by the authorities in at least two countries.

The sound of children at play reached Hannah's ears as she approached the open door of the cottage. Gavin was with other boys practicing their skill with crossbows. Their target, a large mound of straw covered with a tattered old sail, looked like a giant hedgehog. Arrows were protruding in every direction. She waved to them as she caught the scent of fresh baked bread coming from the cottage.

"Good morrow," Betsy's voice came from within the room.

Stepping inside, she paused allowing her eyes to adjust after the brightness of the sun light. "Good morrow, Betsy. The bread smells delicious."

The cottage was homey and spotless. A wood plank table, worn from years of scrubbings, stood in the center of the room with a bench on either side, as was customary. Several shelves mounted to the solid wood wall held trenchers, flagons, and assorted clay jars. The wall at the rear of the room was made of native stone; the fireplace was as tall as Hannah took up the center. A ladder of thick tree limbs led up to a loft. To the left of the fireplace a large leather hide covered a doorway. Steaming loaves, golden and crusty, filled the sill of the open window.

Turning from the fireplace with a smile, Betsy wiped her hands on her apron. Smiling and shaking her head, she reached for one of the clay jars. "With so many mouths to feed, I started baking early."

"May I be of help?" Looking around the room, Hannah wanted to be useful.

"You could slice a loaf of bread." Betsy indicated a knife and loaf on the table, with a nod of her head. "There is fresh butter and honey." She was gathering several of the clay jars into her apron.

Moments later Hannah and Betsy sat across the table from each other. Betsy had prepared the tea for Hannah to drink with all the skill of an apothecary. Betsy drank a tankard of ale as they enjoyed the fresh bread with butter and honey.

Hannah stared into the bowl of steeping herbs floating in a thick brown liquid, reminiscent of mud puddles after a hard rain.

"How soon will this work?" Hannah questioned.

"A day, maybe two, no more. There will be little pain, cramping in your stomach. Then the blood will start and become heavy, and then lessen. The bleeding should only last four or five days, or as is normal for you and your regular courses."

Hannah took a deep breath. She trusted Betsy. In some way uniquely her own, Betsy was a mixture of the housekeeper and her mother. "Will I be able to have other children?"

"Of course," leaning forward she winked at Hannah, "Without this tincture I would have had a bairn every year." She laughed. "We women must have our secrets in this world or we would not survive."

"The longer I am away from my father's manor, the more I realize how little I know of the ways of the world. I have no one to learn from now that my mother is gone. I miss her so."

"You are young. You will fall in love with the right man one day. I do not think your father is a man who would arrange a husband for you." Betsy looked away when she mentioned Edward.

"He may now, if he can get me out of the mess. Father never approved of Thomas. Thomas was my choice. Father was correct and I was so very wrong." Fighting back tears, she tested the temperature of the foul smelling liquid.

"We cannot change the past. We can change our future by learning from our mistakes. You are taking the first step this morning, now you must choose what your next step will be."

Spooning the larger pieces out of the bowl, Hannah willed her stomach to calm. "Thank you for this." She inhaled deeply and whispered, "women's secrets."

She drank quick, expecting it to taste foul, the added honey almost covered up the bitterness. Not unpleasant, Hannah finished the drink, sitting ever still.

"I would like for my next step to begin today by becoming useful. Clan members will be returning to their homes and with the wounded to look after, there must be something I can do to assist."

"My supply of healing herbs is diminishing rapidly. On the morrow, while the dew is fresh, I shall be replenishing my stores. Would you like to keep me company and perhaps learn about them?"

"Yes, I would." Hannah nibbled on her bread. "How did you learn about healing with herbs? Like the ones I was preparing for the wounded."

Betsy leaned forward, her forearms resting on the table. "Many years ago, before my first born, there was a wise woman living just over the hill. All of us went to her for cures when there was sickness. I was searching for a goat that had wandered away and came across her while she was harvesting the wild plants. We talked. She told me about the herbs she had gathered in her basket. She spoke of their healing properties."

Pouring another ale, she continued. "I would go visit her in her cabin as often as I could. She was very wise and I learned from her. Some said she had special powers. Others said she was descended from the ancient druids. All I know is, she was my friend."

"She sounds very kind. Will we be seeing her on the morrow?"

"She died two winters ago. She was the kindest soul I have known. Healing and saving many, she never asked for anything in return. In England she would have been called a witch." There was sadness in Betsy's voice. "I miss her greatly."

"A witch?"

"Yes, a witch. Some called her such. But, for my part she was my friend."

"From what I witnessed last evening, you saved many lives. You relieved the pain and suffering of those injured, making you and your teacher healers and physicians. Many would have died last night if not for you." Hannah stood and stepped around the end of the table. "Betsy, I thank you for your friendship and kindness."

Leaning over Betsy, Hannah wrapped her arms around her shoulders. "I do not know how to repay you for helping me with my situation."

"You are welcome, you owe me nothing. You have done what you must. I think this was a wise decision."

Forcing a smile, she nodded. "How do you survive like this? You must become lonely."

"The ships provide much for us. Liam is most generous. The only need the ships cannot provide is fresh meat. A neighboring clan's man was glad to share with us while Rory was away with Liam. Then, well, he went away. That was when my dear lover taught me the workings and accuracy of the crossbow. We shall not starve."

"What about the loneliness?"

"I must admit, I would treasure another woman's company. The right woman, mind you." Her laughter filled the room. "There is work aplenty to occupy my hands between ships."

"You amaze me. It is almost like having my mother to speak to once again. Thank you."

Hannah left with a growing respect for Betsy. Women's secrets, an odd term, she thought, headed for the long house. Is it possible the secrets of men out weight the secrets of women? Does everyone have untold confidences hidden deep in the dark recesses of their heart? Things never revealed over the course of a lifetime. Perhaps on some occasions they are taken to the grave. She had witnessed Thomas and Phillip's darkest one. Father had them, and they included William, Rory and now herself.

There was Betsy, she revealed one of hers, perhaps there were more. What about Sarah? Surely not Mother? No, she pushed the thought form her. Never having thought this way, the notion mystified her.

Without hesitation, Hannah turned away from the path to the long house and walked to the quay. Her slippers made no sound on the flagstone beneath her feet. The air was crisp and clean, the slight breeze played at tendrils of hair around her face. She headed to the other side of the harbor. The sounds of sailors talking and a few moans from the ones wounded came to her from the small cottages she passed by. Moving closer to the water's edge, she looked into its clear, bright blue depths.

A school of sardines darted first one direction, and suddenly in another. She watched them for a moment. What cause did they have to change direction? Were they lost? Did they think or feel? If they can feel, she understood for they mirrored her life of the past few months. First, she had been headed for France, then a sudden turn to Spain, a change of course and making land in Ireland.

Following the large flat stones she discovered larger fish, below them sea urchins clinging to boulders under the water were visible in detail. Bobbing in the water, a chard board floated, tapping the stone edge of the quay. No other evidence of the damage and suffering from the night before in sight. The sounds of the men faded behind her.

Leaving the Harbor behind, she headed up the ridge, which formed the peninsula. Trees bent awkward inland having survived a lifetime of wind rushing inland from the sea. Leaves and twigs crunched under her feet and the wind increased when she reached the top. Behind her the harbor with its cluster of buildings. Ahead the open sea.

With careful steps, she made her way down to the waves crashing below. She located a somewhat flat boulder to sit on with her feet dangling high above the waves. The spray dampening her slippers and the bottom of her skirt, she could feel the power of the water, each wave as strong as the last gathering the strength to assault the stone underneath her.

"Each time I gather the strength to move forward, I am forced to face another torment." She spoke aloud. "What I have set in motion, cannot be undone. What if I do not survive? It will all have been for nothing. Thomas may have lost the battle against me, but he will have won the war."

Looking to the horizon, she could see England in her mind. The waves grew louder, drowning out all other sound.

"Father, where are you?" she yelled. "I am so very frightened."

Her future ruined, fear of going mad washed over her. With elbows on her knees, and her face hidden in her hands she wept.

Chapter Twenty-Six

William walked out of the woods. He and Rory had been felling trees to make the repairs on the listing ship. Walking to the mouth of the harbor, to his left was open sea and to his right village. Sweat pouring down his face. He pulled off his shirt and wiped it away. Looking to the long house, Hannah walked across the common area, headed to Rory's cottage. His chest tightened at the sight of her.

He cast his eyes away, to the water several feet below the boulder he stood upon. Stripping off all his clothes, he walked to the edge, took a deep breath, and dove into the water. He swam down, down to the bottom; turning upright, he placed his feet on the ocean floor and pushed upward. Hands at his side he kicked, swift and hard. The water rushed past his ears, roaring, boiling, drowning all other sound.

His head broke the surface of the water and he breathed deeply. Shaking his head to get his hair out of his face and eyes, William swam back to the rock, climbing with sure feet; he reached the top and dressed. He sat down with the sun warming and drying his back. His thoughts returned to Hannah. She was so young and beautiful. Over the years, he had watched her grow into womanhood. Now she was his responsibility.

The thought of touching her hair, her face, her lips, and her breasts. Last evening, she sat beside him. Her breasts spilling over the top of her gown. Her breath coming hard while dancing. Her hand warm in his. She was Edward's daughter. "Stop William, this is wrong!"

"Reduced to talking to yourself now, Liam?"

William drew his cutlass. He had not heard anyone approaching. "Bloody hell, Rory! Next time make some noise." William stayed his blade.

"I made no attempt to silence my foot falls." Rory sat down beside William. "You were not aware of your surroundings."

"I was lost in thought," William admitted.

"Tell me, did that thought have anything to do with a certain female?" Rory asked smiling.

"Is it that obvious?" William looked out across the sea.

"Only to someone who knows you as I do. Betsy sees." Rory's smile faded, he paused.

After a moment, he continued, "You care for her, more than you are willing to admit. You hardened your heart after Katie's death. You were a good husband to her."

"She was a good wife. I have not looked upon another woman. That part of my life ended with her."

"But, you are a man still. You have...stirrings, feelings you cannot deny. These things are natural. It is hard to ignore them, harder still to act upon them. You must choose."

William looked at Rory. "What would you do?"

"Alas, it is not I who must make a choice. I am walking my path in this life. You must choose which path you will walk. But, I will say one thing on this great matter." Rory stood, taking his time he stripped down to his small clothes. "You will have regrets for the rest of your life if you do not tell her how you feel about her." He dove into the water.

William laid back on the warm flat rock and closed his eyes. "Bloody hell, I know not what to do." The warmth of the sun and the rock crept into his damp body.

Hannah was his partner's daughter. He should not be having feelings for her other than that of a guardian. Years ago, after the death of Katie, he had locked away his emotions. He never wanted to feel that intense pain ever again. Loving someone with every thread of your being and soul, only to watch them die was more than he could bear to repeat.

His first inkling of these feelings had occurred when he became angry with her as they sat looking out over the harbor. The thought of her blaming herself for what Thomas had done to her was the cause of his anger. Why was he angry? "You fool, because you care for her. Yes, but as Edward's daughter, she can be nothing more. I cannot feel more for her." He admonished himself for his thoughts and taking a deep breath emptied his mind.

William slept a dreamless sleep.

Startled, he awoke to a female voice screaming. Dressing with haste, his hand went to the cutlass. He cocked his head to the side, listening.

Nothing. Breathing slowly, his eyes scanned the harbor and the cottages. He shrugged, "must have been the wind or a dream."

Jaw clenched, he headed for the village to check on the wounded. The number of lives he was responsible for were mounting. Perhaps, the worst was over and he would be able to relax for a while. Either way he knew what he must do where Hannah was concerned.

Chapter Twenty-Seven

Sarah and Hannah spent the afternoon preparing the evening meal. William and Gavin arrived shortly before sunset. With man size appetites, they enjoyed a meal of roasted meat, bread, cheese and ale. The fare was simple but Hannah was learning new skills and she was proud of her newfound likeness of cooking. This was not the manor, filled with servants. Daily tasks kept her mind busy.

She thought of her education, of how unprepared she was for this life style. Here she was learning new things every day, but, there was so much she did not know. In the most basic of everyday tasks, Sarah was much more educated. Sarah had sat beside her throughout all the years of tutoring and learned almost everything Hannah had. Now, looking at this situation Sarah had learned so much more from her mother teaching her simple everyday life skills as a maid. Hannah had taken so much for granted. In her future, she had always seen a servant to take care of the menial tasks, at least that is what she thought. She had been wrong. She had been wrong about so many things. Now she must…

"Mistress," Sarah touched her arm. "Are you well? William is speaking to you."

"I am fine. I was lost in thought." Hannah blushed realizing they were all staring at her. "What were you saying?"

"I will be leaving two days hence. Rory will accompany me and I shall leave Gavin here to assist you. We are finishing what repairs we can with the tools we have to work with. The crewmen that are fit to sail will accompany me to have the permanent repairs completed and then we will return." William looked at her.

"Is the ship safe to sail?" Hannah played with her food.

"I would not want to take her out too far. I believe if we keep land in sight we can make it fine. The captain was the owner, he and the first mate both died. I talked to the crew and neither one had family to inherit the ship, so Charles and I will add it to our humble fleet. If someone appears in the future with a valid claim, I will return it." William finished eating and pushed his trencher away. "Now that most of clan has returned to their homes and we are somewhat alone; I was wondering if we could work on the translations tonight. I would like to make sure the originals delivered and the copies placed in the right hands."

"Yes, I would be happy to. But, with everyone gone, who is looking after the wounded?" Hannah reached for her flagon.

"The ships cook and a couple of the other mates. Don't worry they are in good hands, and Betsy will look in on them." William smiled. "So are you up for the challenge?"

"Of course, however I have lost my penner."

"I think I have a suitable replacement." William turned to Gavin and indicated the door with a nod of his head.

Gavin headed out the door, disappearing into the darkness. Within moments, he returned with a good size wood trunk in his hands. He lifted it to the table beside William, and assisted Sarah in clearing the table.

William opened the trunk and removed its contents. Hannah went about gathering several candles. Once she was sure she had sufficient lighting, she took a seat across from William. The array of articles between then consisted of several sealed scrolls, folded and sealed letters, blank paper and a penner. He laid aside a few broad sheets.

Opening the penner and inspecting the contents, she set them out one by one to her right. The quills she deftly sharpened with the penknife from the box and gave the inkhorn a gentle shake before pouring its contents into the ink well. The ink smelled of sulfur and had a bluish green color. "This will work fine."

"I am sure these are not of the same quality you are used to. I shall look for a new penner while I am away. In the mean time you might ask Betsy if she has any fine feathered birds you can relieve of a few new quills." William moved one of the candles directly in front of him.

"I can just picture me chasing a goose over the entire island of Ireland in the attempt of plucking a quill," Hannah laughed.

William chuckled, "For Queen and country. However, I think it best if you change into your breeches before you begin such a quest."

Hannah picked up one of the sealed scrolls. "If you are going to see these delivered, breaking the seal will be noticed."

"Not if we are careful." William picked up one of the scrolls. "We do not break the seal. It takes some practice but, if you hold it over the candle flame to soften it, being ever so careful not to melt the wax." He explained as he demonstrated. "You can lift one side of the seal with a pen knife." He slid the penknife under the seal, between the wax and paper. With a gentle hand, he worked the knife back and forth until the seal let loose. He unrolled the scroll with the seal still attached to the end.

"When you have finished with the translation, I will show you how to re—seal the original." He handed her the open scroll.

Hannah smoothed the scroll out in front of her to examine its contents. After a moment, she took up a blank sheet of paper and quill and began to translate the Spanish into English. The paper was not of the quality she was accustomed to, it was rough and coarse. With care in forming her letters and words, she soon filled the large sheet of paper and reached for another. Engrossed in the task, Hannah lost track of the passing time. On occasion, her quill would cease to scratch on the paper when she stopped writing to inspect the lines of the missive. The quill would return to the ink well as the proper translation of words came to her.

William continued to open the remaining seals. After he had finished, he poured ale into their flagons and sat back watching her. She could feel his eyes on her and returned her attention back to the paper.

William was standing at the fireplace when she raised her head. "This one is finished." Hannah straightened, placing her hands on her lower back, stretching, and looked around for Sarah and Gavin.

"Is there anything of importance?" William walked back to his side of the table.

"The author did not sign his name, he only wrote 'your faithful servant'. This part is interesting." She turned her translation around for him to see. "The third paragraph, it speaks of a mutual friend of theirs. 'He would care to have friends in the English court. And will pay a goodly amount for the privilege.' A spy perhaps?"

"You are catching on. Well done." William took up the paper and continued to read.

"Why do you and my father do this?" Hannah stood, stretching again.

William laid aside the sheet of paper. "From the moment an heir to the throne is born, they are educated in becoming regent. They are educated in all manner of warfare, politics, and economics. They are prepared for becoming the sovereign. Elizabeth was not, just as her father before her was not prepared for the crown. Yes, she was highly educated. You must remember she was third in line for the throne. It is our duty to assist her in any way possible. If she is not successful, England could end with another war of the roses. There is the possibility other countries could invade. Therefore we do this."

"I thought the Lancaster's and York's were no longer a threat to the house of Tudor." Hannah took her seat and reached for her ale.

"Anyone with a drop of either blood line could claim the throne if they could raise armies and ships to usurp Elizabeth." Waving his hand over the communiqués on the table, "These are insights to what others are preparing to do. With inside information, we can design counter measures to protect the Queen and her realm. Your father swore fealty to Henry VIII and has done the same to Elizabeth."

"But you, you are here in Ireland. You are Irish. What may, or may not, transpire in England, how does this affect you?"

"That my dear is a whole other history lesson," he stated with a flat voice. "But, Elizabeth is the Queen of Ireland as well as England."

"I was too busy with pretty gowns and ribbons when my tutor was trying to teach me about what was going on in the world. Then after mother's death, I was carrying on in her stead with the running of the manor. I paid no attention to what else Father was doing." She reached for another letter. "I will have these ready for you before you sail. It is the only task that makes me feel useful here."

William looked at her for a moment. "You now have the opportunity to view life from an entirely different perspective. You must choose what you are going to do with this knowledge. You can learn from others their ways, or you can choose to continue feeling inadequate. You are here, with us now, because you were the victim. You are not, nor were you ever the cause. You must decide to remain a victim, or take charge of your life and rise to your full potential."

Before she could comment, he continued, "With that being said, I leave you to your work. I bid you good night." He smiled down on her as he stood and he walked away.

Hannah watched him take his leave. He was correct. She could continue as she was, blaming herself or she could learn the ways of everyday life and how not allow herself to victimized ever again.

"Hannah, it is time for you to grow up," she thought. "Adulthood starts here and now".

She dipped her quill into the ink and began the next correspondence. She was determined to finish the translations tonight and then on the morrow she would begin her education anew.

With no idea when her father would come for her and understanding Phillip could still be searching for her. His posing as Thomas still confused her, but should he reach her with the authorities before her father's barrister cleared her of murder charges, the situation could go awry. She must appear to belong here should anyone be watching. Another ruse she must carry through. One of many. When would life return to normal for her?

She took a drink of ale and remembered the secrets of women, wondering if Queen Elizabeth had the same feelings. Forever, her life changed, just as Hannah's was. Was life for some, meant to be one mountain after another to climb, with only small valleys of calm uneventful paths in between? While others never traversed more than a stones through away from their homes, living their whole lives in the relative comfort of their known surroundings. Hannah was in the midst of having had the first, and now experiencing the later. She had to choose whether to make the most of all the experiences that were yet to come and take charge or let others have control.

Without warning, a ball of fur with sharp nails leapt into her lap. A small scream escaped her as she jumped to her feet. Freya's feet scampered with lightning speed to get away from Hannah and to the safety of the tabletop.

"Freya, where have you been?" Hannah extended a hand to the feline as a token of apology. "You find the strangest ways of making yourself known." Hannah picked Freya up and held her in her arms. Freya head-butted her on the chin and began to purr.

Much later, the writing tools put away, she made her way around the long room extinguishing candles, pondering where Gavin and Sarah might be, she settled into a chair beside the dying fire. Freya joined her and kneading her lap without using her claws. She then settled in for the night.

Hannah absentmindedly stroked the cat and let her mind wander as she stared into the flames. The translations were complete. William would take them when he set sail. He knew how to get the copies to her father. Perhaps he would allow her to include a private message to her father. She would ask him on the morrow. A little news as to what was going on to clear her of the charges would be most welcome. Waiting and not knowing was hard.

"Why are you sitting in the darkness?" Sarah closed the door behind her, and adding some peat to the fire, she took the chair opposite Hannah beside the fireplace.

"I have been thinking of how useless I feel since we arrived here. So, on the morrow I will go herb harvesting with Betsy. I need to keep active or I shall go mad." Hannah never took her eyes from the fire. She breathed heavily, enjoying the earthy scent of the peat smoke.

"Are you feeling well?"

"Yes, thank you. However, I am tired. Good even." Hannah stood and carried Freya into bedroom.

Hannah woke to the sound of rain. Standing by the window looking out over the harbor. Fog was creeping over the water, long tendrils slithering their way to land.

"The ship is still here. I think William may wait for the rain to pass before taking a crippled ship out." A gust of wind carried the rain through the window forcing her to pull the shutters closed. Cool dampness penetrated the room. Pulling her wrap tighter around her shoulders, she added more dried peat to the fire. She liked the smoky, scorched dirt smell of the peat as it burned. It was unlike the wood in the fireplaces of her home in England.

"That would be wise of him," Sarah said carrying a couple of baskets from the larder. "From the looks of the sky, we are in for rain all day." Taking a seat beside the fireplace, she pulled her sewing from one of the baskets.

Hannah followed Sarah's lead, taking a seat across from her. "Is this the shirt you started while we were in France?" she pulled a handful of grey linen from the basket on the floor.

"Yes. I did not know how long you were going to wear breeches and thought you would need an extra one."

"I think I shall finish it and give it to Gavin."

Threading a needle, she went to work. She felt Sarah's eyes on her. "Is there something on your mind?"

"I was just wondering if you have heard from your father." Sarah pretended to take sudden interest in her own needle.

"No word has come from him." Shaking her head, Hannah forced herself to focus on her stitches. "I cannot send you home. The officials are searching for both of us. I regret, having involved you."

"I will not leave you. This is my station, and here is where I shall remain."

Forcing a smile, "Thank you," Hannah placed more peat on the fire and returned to her sewing.

"It is nothing," Sarah kept her eyes on her sewing.

The two spent the morning sewing, Hannah lost in her thoughts with the sound of rain falling outside. The rainy day was not unlike others they had spent together in England. There was the smell of peat smoke instead of wood and there were no servants to bring them refreshments but it was a pleasant day nonetheless. Freya made an appearance and curled up at Hannah's feet enjoying the warmth of the fire.

Near mid-afternoon, they set aside their sewing and began preparing the evening meal. Hannah was enjoying their time together with no need to make small talk. They cut up meat and a few vegetables and soon there was a bubbly stew in the cauldron sitting near the fire. Sarah added some herbs and salt when the door opened and William entered with Gavin close behind.

"Something smells good, and I am most hungry." William smiled, removing his cloak and hung it on a peg beside the door. Gavin carried a large basket across the room and made a neat stack of peat blocks beside the fireplace.

"Gavin, I am so glad you have come. I have a gift for you." Hannah went to her sewing basket and produced the shirt. She held it by the shoulders and offered the tan shirt to Gavin.

Gavin turned blushed scarlet, "Thank you ma'am." He took the shirt in his arms hugging it to his chest. Walking to the door he looked down at his gift and with great care, he hung the shirt on one of the pegs near William's cloak.

In a low voice, William smiled at Hannah, "You have no idea how happy you made the boy. Thank you. No one has ever treated him with such care. You amaze me every day Hannah."

It was Hannah's turn to blush. She turned away and assisted Sarah in filling trenchers for everyone.

"I am most honored that Gavin was pleased with my gift. Had it not been for him, I would have had to leave Freya in France." She looked to the fireplace where the cat remained curled up watching the humans. "She has been a great comfort to me and I know that Gavin enjoys playing with her. Besides who is there to make his shirts? I may not know everything there is about living here in Ireland, but I do know how to make a good shirt."

She carried two trenchers to the table and sat them down. Taking a seat on the bench, she reached to pour herself ale.

William took a seat at the end of the table close to Hannah. "Do you find Ireland much different than England?"

"I must admit I found the whole clan arriving here the day after we did a little different. Not to mention this very table turned into a physician's table on the second night. That was quite different. I think I shall learn even more if I remain here." Hannah ate her stew.

"Such as?" William asked.

"Well as soon as the rain stops, Betsy and I are going to harvest herbs to replenish her stores," Hannah explained.

William looked at her and chuckled. "I am most impressed. The next you will be asking to learn how to operate a cross bow and take up hunting."

"Could I?" Hannah's eyes locked on his to see if he was jesting.

"I think it could be arranged. But, it must wait until I return from getting the ship refitted." William nodded his head.

"Speaking of your trip…I was wondering if there is a way for me to get a message to Father?"

"That should not create an issue since I am sending your translations to him." William stood and walked to the cauldron to refill his trencher.

"May I send word to my mother?" Sarah asked.

Nodding, he returned to the table. "Tell Hannah what you would like to pass on to your mother so that she may write it in code along with her message to Edward. I will gladly take the messages with me and see that they are delivered."

"Thank you sir," Sarah smiled. "I only want to tell her that I am well and that I continue to do my duties." She glanced across the table at Hannah.

"You have done your duty above and beyond what was expected of you. Your mother will be most proud of you. Perhaps the rain will end in a day or two and we can be underway. I am hoping to gain news of what is going on in France where Phillip is concerned. The taverns along the docks are always a good source of gossip."

Freya found her way onto the bench beside Gavin, who was feeding her pieces of the meat from his stew, attempting to do so unnoticed but the cat was purring loudly giving him away. Hannah watched, smiling. He blushed and smiled back at her.

"I know that you ladies make a pallet every night for Gavin. And since the rain continues and I am dry and do not wish to get wet again. I was wondering if you might provide a pallet near the fire for me as well." William looked to Hannah for an answer.

"William this is your home, how could you be denied?" Hannah spoke with a start.

"In England it would be unheard of, but alas, we are not in England. I thought it only proper to ask the lady of the house for permission." William bowed his head to Hannah.

Hannah laughed. Gavin looked at the three of them with a look of confusion. Freya chose this moment to go to the door and emit a loud meow. She scratched at the door, Hannah opened it just enough for the cat to make her escape. "I think that you will not like being out there for long."

"Hannah, I have brought these to show you." William pulled a ledger book from inside his shirt. "The stores are being held in the empty cottages across the way. I need a comprehensive inventory of what we have."

Sitting across from him, she watched with interest as he pulled several folded pieces of parchment from the book.

"These are the manifests. Do you know of a way to consolidate these pages into the book so at a glance I may find totals of each item?" He slid all across the table to her.

Reading over the lists, nodding her head, "I can come up with a comprehensive inventory for you. How soon do you need this?"

"There is no hurry. All correspondence takes priority."

"I shall set this up for you soon." Bending her head over the papers, she read them all and put them away. "I will work on these when the light is better."

The remainder of the evening, William and Gavin played cards while Hannah and Sarah picked up their sewing where they had left off. Conscious of the closeness of William, Hannah attempted to appear engrossed in her sewing.

When she could no longer see to keep her stitches even in the fading light, Hannah produced her penner. She spoke in quiet tones to Sarah of the message she wanted to send, and took up her seat at the table. Using the Greek code, she penned a message to Edward asking for news. To Ann she wrote only "Mother, I am well and continue with my duties."

Hannah folded the paper with great care and sealed it with wax, omitting any seal, leaving wax plain so there was no way of tracing it to her or William. Looking for William, she found him asleep. He had taken up one side of the fireplace with Gavin on the other. The rise and fall of his chest the only movement. The corners of her mouth turned up in an involuntary smile; she blushed. Leaving the messages on the table, she made her way to the bedroom with soft steps, finding comfort in his presence.

Joining Sarah in their shared bed, careful not to disturb her, she lay awake for what seemed like hours. Her mind would not slow down, her thoughts of William racing. He had become her protector, provider, and sometimes, a companion. Comparing the men in her life, she found the three of them all different. There was some similarities between father and William. Nevertheless, both were greatly different from what she knew of Thomas. Thomas turned out nothing like he had presented himself to her in the beginning. With a hand on her stomach, she thought of the child. Someday there would be one inside her conceived in love and he or she would bring great joy into her world. But not this one.

Chapter Twenty-Eight

Hannah woke the next morning to find Freya curled up on her feet asleep.

The rain had moved on. Dampness filled the long house in its wake. Someone had banked the fire the night before and Sarah was adding peat bricks when Hannah entered the room.

"You are wearing breeches today."

"Yes. I am going to join Betsy. Her herbs need restocking." Hannah handed Sarah her brush. "I would like my hair braided for the outing."

Without comment, Sarah took the brush and stood behind Hannah as she sat in a chair by the fire.

"Shall I accompany you?" Sarah's fingers made short work of the braid.

"No. I do not know how long I shall be. Stay here and prepare the meals. I am sure Gavin and William will be hungry."

"The ship has already set sail but they were only taking out of the harbor. William said something about anchoring it on the other side of the peninsula. Gavin and I will look in on the wounded this morning. And with your permission I will help him with digging peat. We are using up Betsy's supply and there is a need for more to keep the wounded warm at night."

"Oh." William had left. She looked to the table where she had left the letter. It was gone. She felt a twinge deep in her chest. He had left without seeing her. "Do what you will. I will be fine and will see you back here later."

From the larder she took a basket and headed out the door to meet with Betsy. Her boots were soon soaked from the wet grass and standing water, making squishy noises with each step. Betsy was awaiting for her in the tree line.

"Any signs of…"

"Not this morning." Hannah walked beside Betsy, the damp grass clinging to her boots. I will send word to you when the deed begins."

"Have you told Sarah?" Betsy paused to inspect a small shrub.

"No. I think it best no—one knows of what I have done."

"There is no shame to be had. Many women have done so. Others would have if they had the learning or knew another who had." There was no emotion in Betsy's tone.

"Even so, I prefer others to think of it as nature taking charge." Hannah turned to look at Betsy. "Would you teach me the ways of simples and herbs?"

"I would be most happy to pass my knowledge on to you." Smiling, Betsy handed her a handful of what appeared to be grass. "You can start by tying up these up by the stems with the cord in the basket. Some of what we gather today, I will make into simples, others for cooking. I will add some of the fragrant ones to soap, I will make in a few days. You are welcome to learn about soap making, if you like."

"Yes. I would be most happy to." Continuing to tie the bundles as they were handed to her, she thought of Sarah. "Where is the peat bog?"

With her head, Betsy indicated the direction. "Over the hill. Why do you ask?"

"Sarah mentioned Gavin was taking her to dig peat. I did not know where they were going."

"That is odd."

"Why?"

"Gavin knows he cannot dig peat so soon after rain." Betsy returned to her foraging.

"I am certain that is what she said. Perhaps she was mistaken about going today." Hannah shrugged a shoulder.

"Gavin knows these hills; he is not likely to get them lost should they be going on an outing."

"So, Gavin was born here?"

"No. Liam was lonely after his wife died, and spent the majority of his time at sea. He found the boy aboard a ship, and took him as his ward. They both needed someone and it has been a good fit."

Her head snapped up, Hannah stared at Betsy, jaw open. "Wife?"

"I thought you knew."

Closing her mouth and fighting to regain her composure, she forced herself to breath calmly. "I have known William the whole of my life. I am discovering I have never truly known him as a man."

Bobbing her head in understanding, Betsy sounded thoughtful. "Many years may pass before you can know the depths of another."

Going about the business of tying herbs, and feeling herself blush, Hannah was careful to keep her head down. It would not do for Betsy to see how much she cared for William. "Tell me about his wife."

"Her name was Katherine; we all called her Katie. She was good for Liam and for a time they were happy. She missed England. Liam took her back and she became pregnant. Rory said he had never seen a happier man than Liam." Betsy walked through the brush and into the tree line. Hannah followed.

Hanging on Betsy's every word. Her heart pounded and sweat beaded on her brow though the chill of the morning remained. "How long ago?"

Clipping new growth from a willow tree, Betsy paused. "Would have been six winters past. Katie died of childbed fever in the spring, the boy died within weeks. Liam was sorely grieved. Pain and anger over took him, then in his loneliness, he found Gavin and he began to rebuild his life. I believe the boy gives him hope."

"Oh." Sniffing the twigs before tying them.

"Liam has not been the same until here of late." Betsy turned with an odd look in her eyes.

"Everyone grieves in their own way and time." Tilting her head to one side, "It was so with Father."

Betsy shrugged. "Yes, I suppose it was." She turned and headed for the trail leading home.

Following close behind, Hannah was trying to concentrate on Betsy's explanation of the day's harvest. What each can be used for and the native names. Hannah heard her voice, the words faded into the noise of the birdcalls around them.

William had a wife and child. Both died. When her own mother died, Father locked himself in his room for days. William had been the only person allowed to enter. She too had taken to her bed. The pain of loss was too great for her to endure. She had not only lost her mother, but she felt her father would soon follow, so deep was his grief.

At the burial when the bell tolled, Hannah had collapsed; Thomas was there to catch her. He carried her to bed in his strong arms. He pulled the covers over her and left. She wallowed in her grief, allowing it to take over. She would have remained in that dark lonely state had it not been for William.

Days had passed, William marched into her room, looking as if he had been in the saddle for days, covered in dust. His auburn hair was windblown and he needed a shave. His voice was firm; he stood over Hannah's bed, with his hands on his narrow hips. There was the smell of unwashed maleness about him. He raised his voice to her, demanding she pull herself together and get on with her life. Saying to her that her mother would not want her to wallow in her own self-pity, she had her father to take care of, a house to run, and servants to manage. She had her whole life ahead of her. Then, he had marched out, slamming the door. Hannah had obeyed him.

Now she realized he knew what they were going through, how devastated they were.

"What did you say?"

Betsy nodded and looked towards the harbor. "There's a ship entering the mouth of the harbor, most likely with hungry men on board." Betsy shook her head smiling. "We had best get to our hearths and prepare to feed."

Looking to the harbor, Hannah raised her hand shielding her eyes from the sun. No alarm sounded as it had last time. There was no cannon fire. The ship was friendly. "Is it always like this? Watching and waiting for a ship to arrive?"

"Yes. The course of a woman's life is spent waiting on men in one fashion or another. It is always good to keep busy. Time passes faster that way." She started walking down the hill. "With Liam's return, the harbor will once again be full of activity."

"With Rory away so often, do you get lonely?"

"No. I am happy here. It is a good life. I traveled to England once. Too many people with a lack of honesty, thinking of only themselves. I prefer my simple life here." She laughed.

Comparing life at the manor with what she knew of life here, Hannah joined the laughter. "I understand. I am beginning to enjoy the quiet."

"I am glad of it."

"I will hurry; Father could be aboard the ship. I must change; he cannot see me dressed thus. I must afford him a proper greeting." Waving, she ran to the long house.

Inside, Sarah assisted Hannah in changing, and began preparing more food. Gavin appeared in the doorway smiling from ear to ear with a bucket of fresh, cleaned fish he had caught in the harbor.

Leaving the meal preparations behind, Hannah stepped out searching every face, every man, for her father. He was not among those from the ship. Disappointed, she stood aside and watched Gavin, with the assistance of Betsy's boys, carry the long table outdoor. In less than an hour the table was laden with food from the long house as well as Betsy's hearth.

The cook from the ship was adding to the array from his stores aboard the ship. He was firmly entrenched at the fire pit. Hannah knew this was not the formal gathering of the clan, no formal seating of hierarchy; this was accommodating a large gathering of people that the long house was inadequate to provide. Food was laid out on the tables; everyone helped themselves to the offering and found seating on one of the many benches, logs or a comfortable patch of earth.

Savory aromas filled the air, her stomach growled and clawed inside her like an angry beast being awaken from slumber. Joining the others, she filled a trencher and looked around for a place to sit. Her disappointment in her father, kept her from joining in with the groups of lively conversation. She headed for the long house to have a quiet meal alone.

"Ah, there you are." William's voice came from over her shoulder.

Turning, she discovered William approaching, making long strides with a stranger at his side. The man's own gait matching William's step for step.

"Hannah, I would like to introduce you to a colleague of mine, Martin Frobisher."

Martin took Hannah's hand bowed over it and kissed her fingers. "Your servant," he smiled.

Hannah blushed, "I am honored as well, milord Frobisher."

"To you milady, I am just Martin. Please, sit and finish your meal." Martin smiled down at her.

Leaning in close to her ear, William whispered, "We have much work to do inside." indicating the long house with a tilt of his head. He turned and called to Gavin, "Have one of the boys help you move a table into the long house."

"I will fill a couple of trenchers and see you both inside." Martin walked away.

The night air was cool and smelled of a mixture of wood smoke and food as she fell in beside William. Hannah looked up, the night sky sprinkled with stars; a slight glow in the eastern sky gave promise of the moon soon to arise.

Within minutes, a table was moved inside. William had quietly spoken to Gavin, and closed the door firmly behind the boy when he left.

The three settled in at the table, the two men more interested in the food before them than conversation for the moment. She found comfort in the knowledge William was near. Now and then, she would glance in his direction. He was a man that would never cause her pain intentionally. He had taken great care to keep her safe. Was this from duty to her father or something else? Could he think of her as only Edward's daughter or could he see her as a woman in her own right? Hannah was comfortable when she was with him, but he made her nervous at the same time. She found herself wanting to please him in everything she did. The thought of him being displeased with her was not to her liking.

Hannah remembered the look in her mother's eyes when father would return home from one of his business trips. It was the same look Betsy held in her eyes for Rory on the day they arrived.

I want to see that look in William's eyes when he looks at me. Hannah blushed as the thought formed in her mind. *Thomas had won me over with gifts. I would think less of William if it took gifts for him to show cared for me. Never again shall the devil beguile me. I was a witless fool. How could he ever look to me other than a murderess and Edward's daughter?* The silence of the unanswered question lay heavy upon her spirit.

"Do tell Martin, how did you become a colleague of William?" Hannah broke the silence.

"It is not much of a story, but I will do my best to give you the short of it." He smiled with mischief in his eyes. "At the tender age of nine, I became a cabin boy on my first ship, and discovered the open sea was my true love, even if she is an elemental mistress. I survived many journeys, and spent some time as a captive in Portugal. Once released, I established myself as a merchant, as was my father before me, in Morocco. Alas, the life of a merchant was not the life for me. I met Liam a few years back and only recently joined his great cause. And here I am." Martin bowed his head.

"I see." looking across the table to William, "Any news from Father?"

Shaking his head, "No. However, he should receive our missives by the end of the week. I sent them along with the ship and returned home with Martin."

A knock on the door drew their attention. Gavin entered dragging a trunk half his size. Heaving, with both hands, he emitted a short grunt when the corner caught on one of the flagstones.

"Thank you," William stood and relieved the boy of his burden.

Gavin smiled, turned and left closing the door.

"This contains correspondence I would have you to pass on, should you find value to your cause." Martin raised his flagon.

Pulling several leather pouches from the trunk, William set them in front of Hannah. She opened the top most packet, unable to see, she began lighting more candles, and retrieved her penner and fresh parchment from a small chest set against the wall.

William poured another ale "You spoke of a business endeavor."

Martin grasped his hands in front of him on the table. "You always have gotten to the heart of a subject, no matter what it may be." He smiled. "Since leaving the occupation of merchant behind in Morocco, I have come to the conclusion that both of us may be losing coin with the arrangements we follow at this time. It occurred to me if we had a secure place to store the items we procure and find a buyer for the goods. It would be possible for us to charge higher prices for goods delivered."

"I follow you so far. What do you have in mind?" William asked.

The conversation left little for Hannah to add. With a sharp quill in hand, she listened while copying the first document in her stack.

"A store house," Martin's tone was serious. "In a secure location, such as here, as we accumulate goods, we set them aside until we find a buyer. Then we escort the goods to the buyer who is willing to pay the highest price."

"Hmmm, this is why I have always liked you Martin. We think alike."

The door opened, she turned to see Rory enter with Gavin as his shadow.

"Rory, join us. Martin was just explaining his thoughts of building a storehouse here. He thinks we should hold out for higher prices," William chuckled.

"Do you speak of a building like the one you have had me clearing the land for just past the tree line?" Rory loomed over Martin before taking a seat at his side.

William smiled. "I suppose that is exactly what he is speaking of."

"Well then, since we are already under way, Martin will be willing to join us for a lesser cut." Rory settled in on the bench.

"Details gentlemen, mere details," Martin lifted his flagon. "What are a few percentages between friends?"

Amused with the ease of male conversation, she smiled. Her hand paused over the ink well. They speak as if I am not here. On the other hand, perhaps, as if I belong.

"Edward and I began the plans for building a store house many months ago, so I returned. It has always been Edwards' belief the ruling powers will be doing all they can to make allies for the demise of Queen Elizabeth. He knew that the Irish clans would continue to fight amongst themselves. I have always remained neutral in their plots and intrigue. Ireland is far from being ready to have a native ruler. The clan fathers are too busy thinking of their own personal gain and have not a thought of what is best for Ireland." William shook his head with sadness. "King Donal is most diplomatic however I do not believe that he will ever rule the whole of Ireland. He is too fond of drink, whoring and writing poetry."

Martin nodded his head in agreement, "As King of Desmond he has proved most wise and a strong leader. Nevertheless the MacCarthy septs are growing in force and strength."

Intrigued by what she was hearing of her father's involvement in politics. She drank of her ale and wondered if Queen Elizabeth knew Father was risking everything to secure her throne. Hannah had been born the same year as Queen Elizabeth, and remembered conversations between her parents of Ann Boleyn's execution. There was talk in the years that followed Ann Boleyn's beheading; about her being unjustly accused. She was innocent of all charges, but had died just the same. Hannah did not know if Queen Elizabeth was more like her father Henry VII or Ann Boleyn. She hoped that it was the latter. Hannah knew she could depend on her own father and William. Whom does Queen Elizabeth trust above all others to keep her grace safe and secure? Was Queen Elizabeth aware that she too had Father and William?

"Then we have an agreement?" Martin was speaking.

"It is Edward's hope that you are among those to be counted on," William chuckled.

"Your being the head of a clan does have disadvantages at times. The hills of Ireland do have eyes. Some say ears as well."

"That is why I make it a point to have as many eyes and ears possible, reporting to me and me alone." There was a hard expression on William's face as he looked down into his tankard.

"That, my brother, is why I prefer us to be on the same side!" Martin raised his eyebrow.

Hannah returned her attention to her writing. Caught off guard, her stomach tightened. A fierce grip, inside her lower stomach, twisted. With a sharp intake of breath, she put away the papers and penner.

"Gentlemen, it has been a long day, if you would please excuse me."

"With that I bid you both a good night. Thank you, milady, for a most gracious meal." Martin bowed his head to her as he stood.

"Indeed. Let us take our leave." William stood. "Gavin, fetch Sarah for Hannah."

"Good even," Hannah bowed her head and headed for the sleeping room.

Gavin headed out the door followed by the men. Alone, Hannah gripped the back of her chair; wave after wave of searing pain weakened her knees. Making her way to the bedroom, she leaned against the wall for support and drew up the hem of her skirt, working her trembling hand up between her thighs. She pulled it away, and held it before her face. Blood covered her hand.

It has begun.

Chapter Twenty-Nine

Hannah stood in the center of the sleeping room, unmoving.

"This is what I wanted," she said to herself, gripped with fear and pain.

"Conceived in pain this child shall perish in pain. This is not right in the eyes of God. But, it is too late now. The deed cannot be undone."

"Hannah?"

"I am here."

The rustle of Sarah's skirt told Hannah of her approach. Walking to the bed forced Hannah to hold her breath. Each step sent stabbing tendrils of pain down her legs.

"Dear God, Hannah what happened?" She rushed forward and slipped in the pool of blood on the floor, then yelled over her shoulder. "Gavin, get Betsy quick and then water, lots of fresh water."

"Let me get you out of these clothes and into bed. I have been with you since your first courses began, this is not normal."

She tossed the clothes in the corner.

"It is not my intention to frighten you but, Hannah; you have lost your baby. Do you understand what I am saying? You were with child."

"I know, I know." Hannah slipped under the covers, trying to control her annoyance.

"Betsy should be here any moment. She will know what to do."

"Do? It is too late to do anything. This child was not meant to be nor was it wanted."

"You are just distraught, you do not mean it. How could you not want your husband's baby?"

"Have care, Sarah. You speak too freely. God's teeth, do you not understand? I want nothing to remind me of Thomas. Now go."

With lips pursed, she turned and left.

A sharp, searing pain tore through Hannah's lower stomach, followed by a rush of blood between her legs. The pain faded, and she breathed a sigh of relief. *It is over.*

"Hannah, it is Betsy, may I come in?"

"Yes, please."

"Sarah is outside and most disturbed."

"She does not understand my not wanting this child. God's teeth, I sometimes regret having allowed her to speak freely with me in the past. She now takes liberties and oversteps boundaries."

"I see." Betsy nodded. "What about you, how are things progressing?"

"Moments ago I felt a surge. I believe it is done."

"May I look?"

Raising the covers, Hannah nodded.

"This is good. It is whole. Can you raise your hips? And I can pull this blanket away."

Feeling the blanket slip away, Hannah lowered herself back down onto the bed. "I will have Gavin bury this." She rolled the blanket into a ball. "How do you feel?"

"The pain has stopped. I am weak."

"All you need now is some sleep. On the morrow you will feel more like yourself."

"Thank you, Betsy. I do not know what I would have done without you."

"It is nothing."

"Thank you, just the same."

"What would you have me tell Sarah?"

"Only that I have lost the baby and that I should like to be alone."

"I will stop by to see you tomorrow. Do nothing strenuous and you will be well."

Eyes closed, she lay her head down.

All that remains for me to do is wait for Father and then, then I will start my life anew.

Hannah slept. A single tear slid down her cheek.

Chapter Thirty

The new day found Hannah with quill in hand bent over the parchments from the day before. The raspy sound of each stroke was a comfort to her. Focusing her mind on the task prevented her from dwelling on the past.

On occasion, she noticed Sarah going about daily chores, having little to say. Hannah did not mind; she had nothing to say to her. Although Sarah was several years older than she was, she was still a maid. The events of the night before had brought a change in their relationship. Here again, there was no going back. The past cannot be undone. She forced Sarah from her mind.

Half way through the stack of parchments, the sound of footsteps pulled Hannah away from her writing to find William standing at the end of the table with a look of concern on his face.

"I can see by the look on your face, you know." She felt heat rise to her face. "I am fine and will be myself again in a day or two."

With a sigh, and a weak smile, he waved a hand across the table. "I see you have been busy. Have you found anything interesting?"

"There is something I want to show you. I am not sure, it may be important."

"Show me." He took a seat across from her.

She handed him the parchment.

William read aloud, "*My debt to you is now paid in full. A parcel has been delivered to the great whore's bastard. The resulting illness will be known to all soon.*

I am unwilling to return to court to witness the aftermath. I am too much of a private person to ever desire notoriety. Therefore, I shall not quit my home, preferring to live in piety.

Should you find yourself in need of my service in the future, I tell you now; you will find yourself unknown to me and mine, a stranger outside a locked door, alone in the cold.

May God have mercy on us both."

He shook his head. "With the only signature being a most decorative letter *K*, there is no way of knowing who the author is."

"There is no way of knowing who this was intended for with there being only the letter G on the other side." Picking up her tankard, she sat it down, not realizing it was empty.

Pouring ale for both of them, he looked into her eyes. "Well done. I must place this one in the right hands post haste. The others?"

"They are here." She slid the missives across the table. "Others are mundane things and I must finish the rest."

"If you can assure me of your wellbeing, I will set sail with Martin on the morrow. It is urgent for me to warn our contacts in England of what you have discovered." He drank, never taking his eyes from her.

A smile spread, and once again, she felt the heat in her face. "I am well, and shall look forward to your return with news of Her Majesty alive and well."

"Rory will go with me. You are safe here. No harm will come to you. Gavin will remain behind to aid you with anything Sarah cannot do alone."

"I am adjusting to life here and I do like being here." She paused. "I ruined the beautiful gown you gave me, and the only other one—"

He waved his hand cutting off her words. "I shall return with a trunk full of gowns for you. And hopefully your father will accompany me."

"Oh yes, I would dearly love to see Father."

"Betsy is cooking a deer Rory killed this morning. We will all dine at the pit this evening and then Rory and I will spend the night aboard the ship. We will sail at first light."

With the copies folded into a leather pouch and tucked into his shirt, William took his leave. Hannah watched him walk out the door.

Moving to the chair beside the fireplace, she sat, staring into the flames. They leapt and danced producing warmth that slowly chased away the cold that had seeped into her core. The smell of the burning peat replaced the muskiness of him in her nose.

William had known her for her whole life. He watched her grow from a child into a woman. He knew almost everything about her.

I know him not.

Chapter Thirty-One

The ship sailed on the morning tide, followed by fog rolling down through the trees, engulfing the community. Hannah wandered the long house, aimless. Pausing to peer through a window at the ghostly form of trees wrapped in fog. Dark sentinels of stability standing against the ever moving, shifting mist. Droplets of rain splattered on the windowsill. Hannah closed the shutter against the onslaught of cold dampness filling the room.

Gavin entered carrying an armload of peat bricks. Depositing them near the fireplace, he turned.

"Good day, milady. Is there anything I can help you with today?"

"If you are looking for an excuse to remain inside out of the rain, you do not need one." She smiled down on the boy, "You may stay and keep Freya and I company."

"I would like that." He threw a couple of the bricks on the fire and scooped up Freya.

"Do you know where Sarah has gone?"

"No ma'am. I have not seen her since yesterday."

"Did she enjoy your outing to the bog?"

A frown crossed his face. "I have not taken Miss Sarah to the bog. It is too dangerous after the rain."

"I have made a mistake. I thought she mentioned you taking her."

What could Sarah be hiding? I am not mistaken about what she said. This is so very odd. Perhaps a young man has taken her fancy.

Producing a small ball of yarn from his pocket, Gavin lay on his stomach on the floor, teasing Freya. He giggled at the cat's antics, settling in for a dry afternoon indoors.

Taking up her penner and sorting through the parchments, Hannah began translating and copying. She forced herself to focus on the task and not on Sarah's lie. There would be opportunity in abundance to discover the why of it tonight. The maid must return at some point.

After a time she set aside her ink and quill, her stomach reminded her of hunger with a loud, gnawing growl. Going to the larder, she brought dried venison to the hearth, and cutting it into small cubes, added it to the vegetables in the cauldron.

The aroma of the stew filled the room, teasing her senses. After tasting the broth, she filled two trenchers, "Gavin, if you will pour the ale we can eat. And yes, I have some for Freya."

He filled two tankards and joined her at the table. Eating in silence, she wondered about his parents and if he knew them. Betsy had not mentioned them and she had not thought to ask. She was on the brink of thinking of him as a little brother. The boy needed a mother figure at his age. There was only so much for him to learn in the company of men. When not with William, he was left to his own devices. And from the way he looked to Sarah, she was certain he had romantic feelings for her. The thought brought a smile to her.

Her fondness for the boy had grown every day since he had fashioned the cage for Freya. He was thoughtful, kind, and smart. Eager to please and she knew if she had a brother, he would have been like him. Perhaps one day she would have a son instead. Until then she had Gavin, and was most grateful for his company and friendship.

She smiled, finishing her meal. Gavin was glancing at the parchments on the table.

"It is hard to write?"

"Why, no. Do you not know how?"

Gavin shook his head.

"Would you like to learn?"

"Yes, ma'am."

"Then tomorrow eve I shall teach you how to write your name. It is a good place to begin."

Gavin reached across the table for her empty trencher, beaming. "I will take care of these."

Hannah nodded and took up her quill, pulling the missives to her. "Would you light the candles first? I think I can finish these tonight and then we will have nothing to get in our way tomorrow."

Pulling a candle near, she set to work and lost all sense of time. Startled when the door flew open, she looked up to find Sarah entering, her cloak dripping on the flagstones.

"God's teeth, Sarah. Where have you been?"

"Did you have need of me?"

"No, but it is late and you have been gone all day. Where have you been?"

Removing her cloak, hanging it on a dowel, she cast her eyes down, and faced Hannah. "I have been tending to the wounded. It was not my intention to be away for so long. I beg forgiveness."

Hannah could feel the tension mounting between them. With a wave of her hand, she attempted to ease their conversation. "Go. Change into something dry before you catch your death. Gavin will fill a trencher for you. I do not wish to reprimand you for your kindness to the wounded."

Sarah nodded once and dashed into the sleeping room. Gavin filled a trencher and poured a pint. He picked up Freya and settled down on his bed with the cat curled up on his stomach.

With care, Hannah put away the parchments, separating the original form the copies. Making her way around the room blowing out the candles, she ignored Sarah when she entered and took her place at the table.

Hannah left a single candle burning on the table. "Good even, Sarah."

"Good even, milady."

Several hours later, Hannah pretended to sleep when Sarah slid under the covers. Hannah accepted the change between them, she did not understand Sarah's lack of compassion toward her for not wanting the child.

God's teeth, I do not answer to a maid and her silly notions of life and children. I shall never again be a victim.

The days past, Hannah remembered Betsy's words of waiting for the men to return. Her days were filled gathering herbs and spices, filled the rafters of the larder with their pungent scent. With her most careful lettering, she labeled each and on the back printed the medicinal properties.

Evenings, she spent with Gavin teaching him his letters and praising him when he managed to write his name for the first time. She found herself missing William.

Sarah helped her dress in the mornings and was there to help her change at bedtime. She was noticeably absent throughout the daytime hours. Hannah did not ask how she spent her days and Sarah extended no explanations. They never mentioned the baby or Thomas. She found herself glancing past the harbor searching for sails. Some days she would sit for hours out on the peninsula hopeful for William's return.

This day felt different. A woman's intuition perhaps. Something was different, almost a foreboding feel in the air. Hannah shook it off.

"God's teeth. Stop this nonsense."

Turning, she discovered Freya standing on the table with her head cocked to one side watching her.

"Yes, I am talking to myself. I am not good at this waiting. I want my father, and I want to see William." Tears filled her eyes. "Now I am talking to the cat."

She pulled her cloak from the peg and headed out the door.

"I am going to see Betsy. You can come with me or chase mice."

Chapter Thirty-Two

Hannah found Betsy sitting near the window, knitting. After pouring a flagon of ale for the two of them, Betsy offered her a set of needles and a ball of green wool.

"You have recovered well, I see."

"Yes, my courses ended yesterday. Being house bound has set me on edge. I cannot shake this feeling that something is not right. I could not stay at the long house another minute. I hope you do not mind I came to you seeking solace."

"My dear, you are always welcome at my hearth."

"Thank you. Sarah has not been much company since that night. There is tension between us. She cannot accept my not wanting Thomas' child."

"Her life lies along a different path. She cannot walk the same path you follow because she has not experienced your trials."

"God's teeth. How am I to mend this with her?"

"It will mend itself or it will not. You must have patience with her. Do not force the relationship. Even then, it may never return to what it once was. Why is this important to you? She is, after all, your maid."

Casting on stitches, she thought about the question. "Perhaps it stems from my being an only child. Sarah was like an older sister to me while I was growing up. Her enthusiasm matched mine in preparing for my wedding. Then, when we had to leave England sooner than originally planned, she told me she would have more opportunities in France when it came time for her to wed."

"She even spoke about her fear of our closeness changing once we were in Thomas' home. I told her we would always be as we were. At the time, I thought that was what I wanted. Now she seems to have outgrown the relationship."

"Tell me, how did you meet this Thomas?"

"It was two years ago. Seems like a lifetime but, it was my sixteenth birthday. My parents had taken me to London to celebrate. We were staying in the home of one of Father's business associates on the Thames River. After spending the entire morning with the dressmaker, Mother and I went downstairs for lunch. We were enjoying hot delicious meat pies and ale when Father came walking in with the most handsome young man I had ever seen. He was tall like Father, and of slim build with broad shoulders, and black hair and eyes. His mode of dress was that of a courtier. It was the latest male fashion in London."

Repositioning the ball of yarn, she remembered a time when she was happy. "Father introduced us as his two beautiful ladies and asked how things went with the dressmaker. Mother told him we had not left a bolt of fabric unturned and invited the men to join us. After Father made the introductions, Thomas kissed my hand and…I was in love."

"Ah, young love." Betsy smiled.

"He never took his eyes off me. I am sure I blushed scarlet. I asked him how he knew Father and he explained he was there in his father's stead, due to poor health; he could no longer make the journey, and how our fathers had been business associates for years.

"After that first day, Thomas became a permanent fixture at the manor. He would leave for weeks at a time to conduct his father's business. On the other hand, so I thought, I was always happy to see him on his return and he would bring me gifts, little things; ribbons, gloves or a bit of lace.

"Then Mother died. Thomas asked permission for us to wed. Father came to me; I begged for his blessing. Father was correct; I should have listened to him."

Hannah felt the pain of remembering deep in her chest. The heartbreak of her mother's death, a period of brief happiness followed by the devastation of discovering what Thomas was capable of doing.

"The past can be painful. It is what you choose to do with that pain in your future. You can let it devour you or you can grow stronger because of it. It is up to you."

"I do not know where to go from here." She waved her hand, "I do not mean here in Ireland. I mean here, in my heart."

"Listen to your heart."

"I did that with Thomas and look where I am now."

"Yes, but now you are wiser and stronger. And your heart will not lead you astray, for it knows what the cost has been."

"I have doubts."

"There will always be doubts. You will know what is right for you if you do not stray from your heart's path."

"God's teeth, I pray you are right."

The door opened. Both women jumped to their feet. Knitting needles hit the floor and balls of yarn rolled across the floor.

Rory filled the doorway. "Wife, I am returned."

A myriad of emotions crossed Betsy's face, she ran to her husband.

Hannah mumbled an excuse and slipped out the door, stepping around the couple locked in an embrace of reunion.

"Ah, colleen, you will find a small chest awaiting you. I had Gavin carry it into the long house." He smiled down at her. "Liam should return in a day or two and would like for you see what you can make of the contents."

Her heart beat faster at the thought of William coming home soon and she headed for the long house. The once crippled ship sat nestled at the quay. Men were off loading supplies and their merriment carried on the breeze.

William was coming home.

In the deepening twilight, Hannah sat with quill in hand finishing the last of the copies and translations. Gavin and Sarah had left her to her task earlier in the evening, having mentioned something about the wounded returning to their ship.

Hannah had a growing fondness for the boy and suspected he felt the emptiness of William's absence as strongly as she did. His eagerness to please shone through, while he strutted around the room, doing his part to make sure she was comfortable and had all she needed before he made his departure. A smile crossed her lips at the thought of his providing for her.

Lifting the seal on the last letter with great care in the manner William had taught her, she set aside the penknife and unfolded the parchment. A small square of paper floated to the table. Unfolded it revealed a series of numbers.

"A Polybius numeric cypher?"

Reaching for her penner, she retrieved a small square of parchment, a cypher key she had copied some days before. Placing the two pieces side by side, she shifted in her seat. Freya curled up on the floor under the table using her foot for a pillow. The cat sprang to her paws, spitting and hissing. Hannah leaned sideways, peering under the table.

"What is wrong little one? All is well."

Reaching to pet the cat to reassure her, Hannah drew her hand back. Freya clawed at the floor in an attempt to gain traction and escaped to the sleeping room.

Shaking her head in puzzlement, she straightened, returning to her quill and ink.

"That is most odd."

"Not as odd as finding my wife in Ireland."

Hannah's head snapped around. She froze and all blood left her face.

"You are dead. I saw your body, dead on the floor."

Chapter Thirty-Three

She stood. Rising terror climbed in her throat closing off her air supply. Her eyes scanned the room. Desperation to flee kept her knees from giving way. There was no escape. Thomas stood between her and the door. He held a cutlass leveled at her chest. Candlelight flashed reflecting from the edge of the sharp blade.

"I assure you, madam, I am alive. It was the dead body of poor, dear Phillip everyone on the ship searched for so desperately." Thomas' gaze was steady and cold.

"How is that possible? The knife was in your side, so much blood on the floor." She fought to keep her voice even and calm. Inside she was screaming with fear.

"I was alive when your lover rolled me in that filthy blanket. He made a serious mistake of leaving the knife with me. It was only a matter of cutting myself loose before dear Phillip returned. The knife slipped upward under his ribs with ease. Poor chap died in my arms. It was a simple matter of rolling him in the blanket in my stead." His lip curled up.

"You murdered Phillip?" Her voice was a whisper.

"Would you be surprised to know he was not my first?" His cruel smirk spread. "My dear stupid Hannah, your mother was my first."

The room darkened and began to spin. Her hands trembled, knees grew weak, and pain stabbed her heart. Clutching the table, she slid onto the cold, hard bench.

"No, no, it cannot be."

"Why do you think I insisted on bringing her soup for you to feed to her? I gathered death cap mushrooms every day from the oak grove.

I was most careful not to give her too much all at once. Mixed in soup, they appeared like the safe ones she was ever so fond of."

"Why? Why Mother?" The pain of her mother's death arose anew in her heart. She had spoon fed the poison to her own flesh and blood.

In her mind, she could still see the knife protruding from his side. His blood pooling on the floor of the ship. She felt the urge to plunge it there again, but this time with forethought. With a deep breath, she forced back the thought of rushing him, unleashing every ounce of her anger.

"It was truly brilliant on my part." His voice was calm and gloating at the same time. "You see, my dear wife; our fathers would not include me in their affairs. I was a mere delivery boy. It did not matter to them how I am so much more. They were intent to protect their precious Queen and England. Not once did they offer to include me as one of their spies. Their web is free of charge when they could sell their information for a price. My father has squandered the family's wealth over the years for Queen and country. While he cravenly lived in France, fearing he too would fall into Mary's hands for being Protestant. Such a fool."

She shook her head. "This makes no sense. Why did you kill my mother?"

"It is all quite simple, my dear mad wife. With your mother out of the way, I wed the grieving daughter, and then rid myself of your father." He paused. "You see, now I know who the spy master is and how all the contacts are made. All I have to do is inherit your father's English connections, along with his wealth and manor. My father will see how invaluable I am, and I will have a place in the web they created as a vital member. I will be in a position to restore my family fortune. My inheritance. Along with yours, it will all be mine."

"You murdered Mother, married me, and plan to kill Father. When all you had to do was ask for a position in their spy web." She looked up at the man she had loved; she felt sickened inside. How could she have been so wrong about the evil standing before her?

"Have you gone mad?"

"No." The madness thundered in his eyes. His face contorted and he swallowed hard.

"My dear wife, you are the one gone mad. You murdered poor, innocent Phillip in a fit of jealousy. In a state of shock, I watched my beloved wife kill my best friend. You will now have to stand trial in

France. I will be ever so grieved when they hang my wretched wife." A thin sneer spread across his face. "I will then inherit everything, all of your father's wealth and connections in England."

In the darkness outside the door, she caught site of movement. Someone was there. She dared not take her eyes off Thomas. If she took her eyes from him, he would know. She had to keep him focused on her and her alone. She stood, feeling the pressure of her dagger at her waist.

"Thomas, how did you find me?" She was amazed at the calm in her own voice.

"A most interesting tale." His glare never left her. "I questioned every man aboard the ship that night. As long as the ale flows with another's coin, a man's lips become most loose. One in particular, told of two men along with two boys being the first to leave the ship. There was no doubt in my mind. One of those men was your precious William. The other, they described to be a rather large man.

"For days I searched the inns and boarding houses. Then luck was with me. I visited a particular house of pleasure for a little distraction. There, I overheard two of the servants whispering about guests on the third floor. I slipped up the back stairs and found a hulk of a man guarding one of the rooms. I never dreamed I would find answers about my wife in a house of prostitutes."

Pulling his own knife from its sheath, he brought it to his lips and kissed it. Eyeing Hannah, he smiled.

"Maternal instincts are an amazing thing. Most remarkable when a knife is held to the throat of a child before it's mother."

"No, no. Not Louise's son. Please, tell me you did not kill an innocent child." Bile rose in her throat.

"Why Hannah, do you think me a monster? I assure you the little bastard is alive and well in his mother's arms. His mother, on the other hand, will not soon forget me. The whore forgot to mention you crept out the alleyway as we spoke. She will carry the scar across her face for the rest of her life." He began to laugh.

His laughter sent a chill up her spine. She must not be ill now. To show weakness would only add fuel to his cruelty. Forcing herself to swallow and willing her hands not to tremble, she reached for the ale, drank deeply. With the tankard blocking him from following her eyes, she dared to glance out the door.

There is someone in the shadows. God's teeth, who? Was someone with Thomas? If so, she had no hope of escape. Rory returned hours ago. Sarah and Gavin should be home by now. Lowering the tankard, she replaced it on the table, and forced her hand steady.

"Wife, where are your manners? Are you not going to serve your husband?"

The sound of his voice put her teeth on edge. She poured ale for them both. Pushing the parchments aside, she placed his as far away from herself as she could reach.

"And then?"

He downed the ale. "And then your trail went cold. I spent weeks searching. Weeks, Hannah, searching for my beloved wife."

He glared at her. "With a list of every ship sailing from the day you ran away from me, I searched. The local authorities were incompetent, less than useless. Then I heard the story of a ship drifting ashore. Pirates had overtaken the ship.

"The crew was very eager to tell their tale, with details of pirates with strong Irish accents. Their cargo taken, and of how two men with a price on their heads were discovered. Their descriptions fit William and his giant. Only this time, not two boys, but a boy and a woman accompanied them.

"I set sail for Ireland, heard the news of a Liam returning to his clan with a large man called Rory and two women. One was none other than my beloved mad wife." He indicated the empty tankard sitting on the table. "It is a small island and news travels fast."

Careful to stay out of the reach of the cutlass, she refilled his tankard.

Freya leapt on the table, spitting and hissing at Thomas. He swiped at the feline with the blade. The cat flew into the air and disappeared under the bench.

"Bloody beast."

Fearing he would do the pet harm, Hannah attempted to keep his attention on herself. "What happens now that you have found me?"

"You are charged with the responsibility of producing an heir before you hang. There can be no solace otherwise." A contorted smile crossed his face.

A shiver ran down Hannah's spine as she held his gaze.

"You will live long enough to provide me with a legitimate heir to the Bingham estates, and then, my dear, I will be rid of you once and for all."

Rage filled her in a wave of heat. Her hand went to her waist.

"You have already planted the seed of your demon spawn in my belly. I have rid myself of your child before it could be born. There will never be another."

Freya flew across the table hissing and spitting, and hurled herself at him, teeth bared, and claws extended. Thomas turned throwing up his arm to protect himself from the cat's attack.

Hannah drew her knife, stepping forward, her eyes on his lower chest. She clenched the handle so tight her knuckles went white, her face set in determination of the deed at hand. Grief and repulsion gave her the strength required as she brought the knife close to her side ready to plunge the blade deep up under his ribs and up through his cankered heart.

Before she could follow through, a whizzing sound startled her. She followed his gaze down to his chest, a bolt protruded through his doublet. Astonishment crossed his face. Lowering his cutlass, his free hand raised to touch a drop of blood that dangled from the tip. He frowned. His body wavered and fell against her.

Revolted, she shoved him away and watched as his body twitched, a heap on the floor face down.

"This does not end here." He gasped for breath, lips drawn up in a hideous smile. I shall be avenged, my sister lives still."

His maniacal laughter filled the air, followed by a terrifying scream from the darkness outside.

Her hands flew to her ears to block the sounds.

Weakened arms attempted to push the weight of his body upward. Blood spilled from a thin line on the middle of his lower lip. He fell forward. In an attempt to speak, a cough emitted a spray of crimson splattering on the hem of her dress and on the floor. His hand slithered across to grasp her ankle.

Instinct took over. She kicked him away and stepped back.

He coughed hard and spat up more the hot, red liquid before he collapsed and wheezed with the petty attempt of breathing before he went quiet. Blood pooled around him and his eyes drained of their light and color.

Betsy entered the room, a crossbow in hand. Gavin followed in her wake, dragging a sword behind, the length longer than his height. He pushed forward, struggled to manipulate the hardened steel around with the tip resting on the still body bleeding on the floor.

Sarah ran past them and came to a halt a few feet from Hannah. The color drained from her face, "Hannah, you are wounded."

Hannah bent her neck down. Scarlet red blood was spreading across and down from a hole in the left side of her bodice. Thomas had taken advantage of the moment. Even in the act of dying he attempted one last time to end her life, he had pierced her through her gown. Focused on surviving, she had felt nothing. She put a hand to her side, touching the red liquid seeping from her own body, mixing with what remained of Thomas on the floor. She held her hand up. It was covered with blood, her eyes locked onto her maid's pale face.

"Sarah…"

Darkness engulfed her.

Chapter Thirty-Four

Wrapped in the arms of a great mist, she floated across the land, engulfing all in a silent embrace of fog. Searching. Searching for William. He must know she did not kill Thomas. She was free. She must find William before the depths of the mist carried her away to be lost in despair for eternity.

Faces floated before her. Voices calling. In desperation she held out her hand, her fingers extended to touch the face of William. Then he was gone. He was near. She could hear his voice.

"Hannah, open your eyes. I command you to open your eyes. You are my great desire. Should there be anyone to blame for this, it lies at my feet. I should never have left you. I swore never to take another wife but, if you will only awake, we shall wed and you will be happy all the days of your life. Just open your eyes."

"William?"

"Yes, Hannah, I am here. Do not attempt to speak, only listen. We know of what has taken place here since I left. Be assured no one will ever hurt you again. You are safe. Your father has sent word to the authorities in both England and France of the foul deeds done."

"Father is here?" She felt the warmth of his hand holding her own.

"He is with Rory and Betsy. Before I tell him you are awake, I must ask you a most serious question. Listen with care, I must know. Could you ever love a man like me?"

Never had she heard his voice soft and tender as she did in this moment. Her eyes closed and she opened them again. He is here, holding her hand in his.

With a weak smile, she looked up into his face. "What folly could ever prevent me from loving you with the whole of my heart?"

William inhaled deeply. "Then live my love that we may become as one heart."

She felt his hand slide under her head. He turned her face to his. He drew close and he kissed her. An unfamiliar warmth moved throughout her body from her head to her toes. William's lips were surprisingly softer than anything she had ever felt and it was magnificent. This kiss was unlike that which she shared with Thomas, his being cold and hard just as his heart had been. Though William was a large, rugged man, his movements were gentle and tender.

Hannah moved her other hand to hold the back of his head and William's hand cupped the side of her face. Her heart was pounding inside her chest, the feeling should have been painful, but the only thing she felt was bliss.

Was this what love was like? Was this the feeling that came when you loved someone who loved you in return?

Their lips parted, she took a soft breath and opened her eyes, peering into William's brilliant green ones. She could tell from the glimmer of happiness in the emeralds she gazed into that he felt as she did. A smile spread across her lips and she gave a happy giggle.

Pulling away, William grinned, and heat rose to her neck and face. "I heard voices."

"Father." Hannah attempted to rise and winced from the stabbing pain in her side. Her father stood behind William.

"Are you well my daughter?"

She noticed the worry in his voice. "Truly, my body shall mend and I shall be whole again. I come from healthy, strong stock."

She smiled in an attempt to reassure him and tears filled his eyes.

Withdrawing from the chair, William's eyes never left her as he bowed his head. Edward was quick to take up the vacated chair and took her hand in his.

"I cannot bear the thought of losing you." He leaned forward and kissed her forehead. "Not being able to see you with my own eyes, I have worried terribly."

Hannah wept tears of relief and joy, both melting together.

"Do not cry my dear. William filled me on the details when he met me in Dublin. Betsy told me the rest when we came ashore. It is all over now. You have nothing to fear. As for Thomas, I have sent letters to his father, the English and French authorities, and this travesty has ended. Once you are healed I shall take you home."

"But there is more. Betsy and Sarah were too far away to hear

Thomas's final words. I am afraid a threat looms still."

"No, my poppet. Thomas is dead and his plot died with him." He squeezed her hand.

Frowning, William placed a hand on Edward's shoulder. "Let her finish. What did he say?"

She opened her mouth. The words caught in her throat, tears filled her eyes. The memory of watching a man die at her feet flooded her mind. The smell of the blood as it spread across the floor. His hand touching her foot. The sight of his eyes going dim as his life ended. She wanted to scream.

"Get her a flagon."

William wheeled from the room.

"Breathe and calm yourself. You are like your mother in so many ways. She too could not speak when she was distraught."

Returning with the ale William sat on the edge of the bed. With one arm, he helped her to sit. With the other, he pressed the pint into her hands.

"Drink slowly and take your time." Tenderness tinted his voice.

She did as instructed. Holding the flagon firm, she let it rest on her lap. With a deep breath and eyes closed, she forced the words to come.

"Thomas was on the floor. Betsy's bolt was protruding through his chest. He was laughing. There was so much blood. On the floor. On me. He laughed and said 'This does not end here. I shall be avenged, my sister lives still.' He grabbed my foot. He touched me as he lay dying."

"Sister? Edward, what is she talking about?"

"I know nothing of a sister."

"That is what he said. 'My sister lives still'".

Edward stood and ran a hand through his hair. He began to pace. Hannah watched in silence.

"In all the years I have known Robert there was never a female child. He had his dalliances, as was his nature, but, I know nothing of any bastard being born."

"Is it possible this is only another method of upsetting Hannah?"

"I do not know. There is only one way to find the underlying cause of this. I must go to Robert. I shall return the body of his son and question him. If there is a sister, he will tell me one way or another. Either way, I will put an end to this. I believe we should remain cautious. If this sister exists and she is a threat we have no way of knowing where she may be."

"She may be in league with someone as well." William stepped closer to Hannah.

"Yes. There are too many variables. I do not want this new information to leave this room."

"That is wise. We are somewhat isolated here but news does have a way of getting out."

"I shall set sail at first light. If the wind is in our favor I should be in France by night fall."

"Then I shall take my leave of the two of you and make ready the ship." William bowed his head, turned and left.

Edward returned to the chair at Hannah's side.

"Do not worry yourself about this. William will keep you safe until my return."

"Yes Father." Hannah laid her head back. His words were reassuring. Nevertheless, fear crept up her spine causing a chill to fill her insides. She attempted to steady herself, placing both hands on her stomach.

"On a lighter note, you must be famished. Betsy and Sarah have prepared a feast. I shall go acquire a trencher and feed you myself." He smiled and stood.

"No, Father, send Sarah to me. I shall join you with the others." Hannah gritted her teeth and pushed herself up.

"Are you certain you are strong enough?"

"Yes, Father."

"As you wish, my dear." He kissed her forehead again and left the room.

Within the hour, Sarah had added extra padding around Hannah's wound and laced her loosely into the new burgundy gown Edward had brought to her from England. Sarah was also in a new cream-colored one. Hannah refused to lean on Sarah when she entered the larger room with her chin held up.

William stood near the fireplace and took her arm. He guided her to a chair near the head of the table and poured an ale. She drank while he remained standing protectively behind her chair, one hand resting on her shoulder. Her father stood across from her conversing with Rory. Gavin and Sarah scampered to place the last of the foodstuffs on the long table.

From the shadows of the doorway stepped Betsy, adorned in a new russet gown as beautiful as Hannah's own. When she approached her husband, Edward turned to greet her. His arms spread in welcome, he took her hands in his, "Dear sister, how goes it with you?"

Betsy beamed. "Brother, I—"

Hannah choked on her ale, spewing it across the table. "Sister? Brother?"

Everyone in the room stared at Hannah. Edward turned to Betsy. "You have not told her?"

"No. When I realized she did not know, I thought it best if she learned from you." Betsy's face was serious.

Edward smiled down at Betsy. "Come, join me at the table and we shall tell her together."

With Edward across the table from Hannah, Betsy took a seat next to him. Rory sat next to his wife and began carving large portions of wild boar. Sarah and Gavin were quiet while they began serving.

All the while, Hannah sensed William's eyes on her. She drank more ale and waited for the explanation to begin. Was there no end to the secrets Betsy held in silence?

"Your grandfather, my father, was known to have many mistresses. My mother pretended not to notice, of course. He fell in love with one. Betsy's mother. Their liaison lasted for several years and Betsy is the result of their love." He voice was calm and soft with affection.

"She was born a few years after I. Knowing he could never marry Betsy's mother, he arranged a good marriage for her within the clan O'Murphy."

Rory engulfed Betsy's hand in his.

"Father sent money every year for the care and needs of his daughter. After he died, I continued to send money to Betsy. She is my only sibling and I chose to take care of her as such." Edward reached for his ale.

"Dear brother, my life has been good here. My mother's husband was kind to me. He treated me as a beloved daughter even after Margaret was born. I am now most happy in my marriage and have sons of my own." Betsy smiled at Rory.

"But Margaret O'Brady is your sister." Hannah thought of the overbearing, bitter woman she had met the day of the welcome feast.

"Yes, but we are nothing alike." Betsy gave a wicked smile. "And Edward, thank you for my gown, it is beautiful."

"You are most welcome, sister." Edward took her hand and kissed it.

Tankards and trenchers filled and small talk spread through the room. Hannah watched the people who were most important to her all gathered in the same place. She pushed the pain in her side to the back of her mind and smiled.

Too much transpired today, she needed time to process the whole of it. She loved William and he returned her love; wanted them to marry. She sensed his eyes on her now. Warmth rose to her cheeks and she toyed with the food in front of her.

What will Father do? He said *we* would return to England. Did he include William in 'we'?

In addition, now I have an aunt. I have grown fond of Betsy. She helped with my little problem, never condemning. Then cared for my wound.

She reached for more ale and glanced across the table. Betsy was laughing at some jest between Father and Rory.

I cannot think of all this now. She reached for more ale.

"I hear music coming from the fire pit. Could it be the sailors play music as well as they handle a ship? I would like to dance with my sister." He leaned his head forward to see Rory. "With your permission, of course."

"Of course." Rory smiled as brother and sister rose from the table.

William placed his hand on Hannah's shoulder, keeping her in her seat. "You are not walking anywhere."

He nodded to Rory and the two of them carried Hannah in her chair out of the long house.

Unable to stop herself, Hannah giggled and caressed William's hand when, with care the two men placed her near the fire pit beside a table laden with flagons full to the brim.

The ale flowed and merriment abounded. A great weight had lifted from them all now the nightmare of Thomas had ended. Her intuition tugged at her of a new threat slithering her way to hamper their happiness.

Hannah watched the dancing. She grew tired, but said nothing. Fear or dread still weighted her down. Her hand slid down to her side. There are wounds and there will always be scars but tonight the panic that had gripped her for months was gone. What remained may or may not be as awful as the past.

William never left her side and the warmth of his hand resting on her shoulder. With the knowledge she would always be safe from harm with him at her side, she said a silent prayer of thanks. Looking up at his face, their eyes met and she warmed deep inside. The thought of his lips on hers made her grow hot and she turned away.

All was in good cheer when the dance ended and Rory claimed his wife for the next. Edward approached the table. Reaching for his pint, he took a long drink.

"William, walk with me for a time. There are a few things we must discuss."

"Of course." William followed Edward in the direction of the quay.

Hannah watched them disappear into the darkness. The two men she loved most, walking side by side into the night.

***

Edward walked in silence. The dark of the moon left little to view. The waves lapping against the quay and the two ships tethered nearby, aided Edward in his course of direction. He felt the need to be far from the ears and eyes of those who might remain aboard.

It was William who broke the silence.

"I have failed you. And I have failed Hannah."

Edward stopped, turning to William he spoke in soft tones. "You have taken great pains to keep my daughter safe."

"That is the point. I did not keep her safe. Since we sailed from England she has had two attempts on her life." There was pain in William's voice.

"She is alive. Her body will mend. You have not failed either of us. We will speak of it no more." Edward was firm.

"I wanted to speak to you about the letters Hannah has been translating and copying. They do not seem to be of much importance, but they have been. There have been many attempts on the Queen's life. Walsingham discovered many messages inside the ones you provided. They appear at a glance to be normal correspondence of family matters, illness and the like. Some were references to the attempts on the Queen herself. Poisoned food, poison disguised and hidden in gifts. Her Majesty sends her deepest gratitude to you and Hannah."

He watched as William began pacing back and forth in front of him. He continued, "Francis has made it to court, he will soon replace William Cecil as Secretary of State. He has set a most trusted man in the service of the Bishops. There are those who support Mary Queen of Scots and they would see her usurp Elizabeth.

"I think I may have a solution as to having more eyes and ears in court. After I clear up this business of Thomas saying his sister will avenge him, I shall send Hannah to court. The Queen has stated she will be most welcome. Having her as lady-in-waiting will give her the opportunity to go where men cannot."

There was no response from William. Edward watched him pace, and realized he was not listening. "Bloody hell, William, have you not heard what I have said?"

William stopped, and turned to Edward, took a deep breath, opened his mouth, clenched his jaw and closed it again.

"Edward, I ask for your blessing and permission to wed Hannah."

Chapter Thirty-Five

Under a dark moon, two men stood on a quay in County Wexford on the south-eastern edge of Ireland. Their conversation involved a woman, a woman with a past. One wanted to wed her, the other intended to return his daughter to England and send her to Queen Elizabeth's court to spy for Francis Walsingham.

Edward had never seen this behavior from William.

"William, Hannah is my beloved daughter. Nevertheless, she is now damaged goods. Some will whisper about her at court. Others will try to take advantage of her past. You cannot be serious about wanting to marry her."

"Over the past few months I have watched her as she survived what would bring most men to their knees, none of which was her fault. Hannah has grown into a strong, beautiful woman and she deserves a man who will love her for who she has become not in spite of it."

William clenched his jaw. "You let your spoilt daughter marry the boy of her choice. That did not work out so well. Now contract her to a man. One she deserves, one who loves her. I am that man."

"Think of what you are saying. Your wife died in childbirth, now you want to take another with a past. You are the head of the clan. They would never accept her. I know. Mine own half-sister married into your clan. This would cause dissension that could tear apart County Wexford. No, I cannot allow this to happen. Not even for my daughter." He turned away from William to gaze on the gathering around the fire pit. The music and dancing continued in their absence.

He turned back to face the harbor. The wind picking up the smell of rain salted the air. "Had you asked for a marriage contract a year ago, I would gladly have given you my blessings. Now, it is too late. Too much has transpired." Edward shook his head.

"You are wrong, and you are wrong about the clan, about Hannah and about me. Yes, I am the head of the clan. They know why I had to leave and have accepted my return. They have accepted Hannah. They accept her because of who she is as an individual. She proved herself to them the night she stood side by side with Betsy tending the wounded. Elbow deep in blood and gore, not once did she turn away. She stayed the course and saved lives. The clan accepts her because she is your daughter as well. When she is my wife they will grow to love her as I love her."

"You would risk everything for Hannah because you love her?"

"Yes."

"I have been waiting to hear this from your own lips." Edward paused. He wanted his words to sink in. He stood toe to toe with William and waited. He knew the man well. By his stance, he was angry. With his anger, the truth of his emotions had come to the surface.

"Betsy told me you had the look of love on your face every time you were with Hannah. She did not know if you knew you loved her." Edward paused again. "I needed to know that you knew, to know that the next man I gave my daughter to would truly love her."

"I did not think it possible to love again. It has been a torment to my soul, to think of Hannah as anything other than your daughter. However, she has proven herself more. Realizing I loved her, I was fearful of it." William paused and took a deep breath. "Edward, are you now saying that I may take your daughter to wife?"

Edward placed his hands on the other man's shoulders. "Yes, that is what I am saying."

William walked away, turned, and marched back. "How shall we proceed?"

"You sound as giddy as a boy in short breeches." Deep laughter rolled through his body. "I will draw up the contract tonight and leave it with you on the morrow. I want you to be the one to inform Hannah. Now let us return to the festivities, before I retire to the ship."

"Thank you, sir."

"Did you hear any of what I said previous to your proclaiming your love for my daughter?"

In the darkness, William stammered. "Well, sir, I heard something about Walsingham returning to France and informants being strategically placed in England. It was when you mentioned your intentions of sending Hannah to court that I stopped listening."

Edward laughed. "That is what I thought!"

He slapped William on the back and the two men walked together back to the fire pit as the sound of bagpipes filled the air.

Chapter Thirty-Six

Dawn was slow to break in County Wexford. Thunder rolled across the hills. Lightning crackled in the sky. Hannah could feel the reverberation pounding in her chest, sitting across from William in the long house. She worked with diligence on transcribing the letters before her, refusing to remain abed. Candles flickered and the scent of tallow mixed with peat smoke and pungent ink filled the air. William worked on the business of providing Queen Elizabeth with the Irish whiskey she was so fond of and a full page contract.

Setting aside her quill with a deep sigh, she straightened.

"I cannot do this now."

William's head snapped up.

"Are you in pain?"

She saw the concern in his face. "Yes. But, that is not the cause of my anxiety. I cannot get Father's trip out of my mind."

Placing a finger to his lips, he stood and without making a sound walked to the open window, turned his head in both directions and returned to the table.

He nodded his head for her to continue.

"I do not fear this possible sister as much as I once feared Thomas but this not knowing, I fear I shall go quite mad."

"Again, we shall have to wait for your father. There is nothing else to do. He is the only person who can get to the bottom of Thomas' threat."

"Yes, I know. But I feel as if this nightmare will never end."

"Then perhaps you need a change of duties."

"A change of duties? William I can barely walk across the room without pain stabbing through my side. Betsy comes and changes the bandages, applies her paste, and has me drink her foul-tasting brew. And I sit here writing. What else can I do?"

"Perhaps look forward to a wedding." He pushed a sheet of parchment in front of her.

Her eyes went from the paper to him and back again.

"Is this…"

"Go ahead. Read."

Picking up the parchment, she recognized her father's bold lettering. Her eyes scanned down to the scrawled signature of William's hand.

"This is a marriage contract. When did you have time to speak to Father?"

"Last evening when we walked quay side. It was either marry you or he was going to send you to court." William smiled, rose, walked around the table to her side, pulled her to her feet, and enveloped her in his arms. "You manage to get yourself into enough trouble on you own without all the drama of currying favor. So I thought you would be better off here with me as my wife."

The tenderness with which he held her was everything she had imagined she would find in Thomas' arms. This was so much more. She lifted her gaze to meet his. Never had she seen any man look on a woman with love and yearning as she saw before her. Her throat tightened and words escaped her.

"Unless of course you have changed your mind," he teased.

Still unable to form words she shook her head.

"That is what I thought." He tightened his hold on her, his head tilted and his lips sought hers.

The warmth of his embrace cradled her. She returned his kiss. His manhood became hard against her and panic filled her, battling the yearning inside her. The painful memory of her last encounter with intimacy caused her body to stiffen with fear and doubt.

He pulled away from her reaction, and stepped back.

"I apologize. I forgot myself. This is unfitting of me. I apologize, please forgive me."

Finding her voice, she shook her head. "No. It is not you. Memories of, of Thomas, and I, I just cannot seem to force them away."

"It was stupid of me. I know better."

"Please wait. You do not understand. I do want to marry you. I love you. Moreover, this time I am sure of my love. You are not Thomas and I know that. I am frightened of the memories never going away. I am afraid I will not be able to forget what he has done."

"It will take time. I am willing to wait for as long as it takes for you to be able to give yourself freely to me. Never forget that."

"Everything that happened on the ship, his body lying on the floor behind where you stand, it haunts my dreams. And sometimes my waking hours if I do not keep focused on something else."

"I do not know how to make the pain and fear fade from your mind. If I could, I would place my hands upon your head and drive him out of your thoughts forever. That not being possible, what I can do for you is help you to remember you are safe. I pledge to you, I will give my last breath to protect you."

She lowered her eyes. Mindful of the remnants of blood stains on the floor at his feet. A part of her wanted to rush into his arms but her fear sealed her own feet in place.

"I thought of going home for a time. Thinking a change would help. But his memory would be there waiting for me. And Mother, I would not be able to escape him after knowing he is the cause of her death." Her throat constricted, no other words would come.

He reached for her hand, brushed the back of it with his lips.

"Once we are wed I shall take you on a wedding trip. We will sail where there is no memory of him. To Spain, Italy, even Greece. We will make new memories, joyous memories. We will not return until you are ready."

"You would do this for me?"

"Yes. It grieves me to see this great disturbance in you. Frame your mind in the knowledge that you are my beloved."

"A most unusual man you are indeed." She smiled.

"Every person I have met and every step I have made has made an imprint on my life. I am the only one who sees life from this perspective. Just the same, you are who you are because you have survived all that has befallen you in the course of your life. Therefore we are destined to be together as one."

Her heart softened, tears filled her eyes.

"My father looked upon my mother as you look upon me at this moment. I have waited the whole of my life to experience the gift you have just bestowed on me."

"Then you will sail the world with me?"

"Yes."

Chapter Thirty-Seven

Days passed into weeks and still there was no word from Edward. Hannah grew stronger with short walks to the quayside and back to the longhouse. She spent the majority of her days deciphering codes and transcribing the neverending stack of parchments brought to her from the endless flow of ships. Still not one word from her father.

Evenings found William and Rory bent over a chessboard while she sat quietly sewing. On occasion, William would invite her to join him in a game. She enjoyed their time together. Her life was good.

In her dreams, it was a different story. Thomas's corpse walked through her nightmares, his bloody body haunting her at every turn until she would wake screaming or Sarah would awaken her with a shake. Left sitting in her bed drenched in sweat, she would find William standing in her doorway. Day or night, he was never far away.

Though she was wrong in the past, she believed herself safe apart from her dreams. On occasion, she would find herself gazing out the window, willing her father to return with the news of a lie, an empty threat that did not exist.

On the morning of the fourteenth day since he sailed, she left her bedroom dressed in boy clothes.

"I cannot abide another day sitting here. I am meeting with Betsy in the meadow to harvest herbs." She filled a trencher of pottage and joined William at the table.

"Are you strong enough for such an outing?" He raised his head from the ledger spread open in front of him on the table.

"The walk will do me good. I am worried about us not hearing from Father. I need fresh air and to feel the land beneath my feet. The smell of cut herbs will soothe my spirit."

"Your nightmares were lessened last night. Perhaps an outing will do you good." He closed the tome.

"Betsy thinks the same."

"Then I shall go see to the progress on the storehouse. Rory says it is almost finished."

"If you should hear from Father or he returns, please send Gavin right away to fetch me."

"Certainly." He stood and headed for the door. Turning back, he smiled. "Do not drain yourself and I will meet you back here midday."

"I shall be fine. Have you seen Sarah?"

"Not since last evening. Gavin is with the boys fishing off the point on the other side of the bay. I think he is keeping them from under Betsy's feet."

"They are good boys. Betsy has longed for a girl child. She is still hopeful."

"It is good to hear the laughter of children roaming the cottages." He grinned and turned to leave, but stopped in the doorway. "A ship approaches."

She was at his side, breakfast forgotten.

"Stay here out of sight. We have no idea who may be on it. Should your father be aboard, I shall bring him here at once."

"Of course."

He closed the door behind him and was gone.

Curled up by the hearth, Freya lay sleeping. Hannah took a seat on the floor next to her, her mind racing with possibilities and what ifs. She stroked the cat, the sound of men shouting floated on the air. Several moments passed before anyone stepped ashore.

Father had been gone much longer than any of them had anticipated. Would he bring ill-fated news or would his report be in their favor? God's teeth, how many more trials must she endure before she could live without fear and be happy?

"Freya, once this is over I shall never again be afraid, hide, or run. Never."

The feline tilted her head to the side and yawned hugely.

The door opened. Her breath caught in her chest.

Edward stepped into the room followed by William. She launched herself across the space between them and into his arms.

"Daughter, I am weary from my travels. Have mercy on an old man and pour a pint for us all."

Releasing him, she nodded. "Forgive me Father."

She did his bidding as William closed the door. The three sat at the table. Her eyes never left her father.

He drank deeply.

They turned when the door opened and Sarah walked into the room. Slamming down his tankard, Father bellowed, "Leave us."

Startled, Hannah sat back in her chair. The maid turned and ran from the room back into the sunshine, pulling the door closed.

William raised a brow in question. Shrugging a shoulder with a slight movement, she turned back to her father.

"I was too late. I arrived only to discover Robert died that very morning. As you can imagine, the Lady Sollinger was most distraught. Her husband dead, his body not yet cold, then I arrive with the coffin carrying her only child. The best solace I could offer her was to stay and arrange for a double funeral.

"Alas, she was of little help. Other than telling me Robert had a bastard child in Binghamshire and he had vowed to her the child would never set foot on French soil at her behest. This leaves me with no choice other than continue on and return home. Somewhere among our mutual friends there has to be one who know the identity of this sister.

"I shall not rest until I have found this bastard and learned her true intentions. Until that time you shall remain here." He raised his eyes to meet hers.

Her hand found his and she squeezed.

"Stay a while and rest, Father."

"No. I shall see this through to the bloody end. This evil young man has destroyed my family. I will not take any chance of a remaining threat."

William stood. "Very well, stay with your daughter. I go to ready the ship and will return when she is prepared to sail. The sooner the better, less chance of anyone learning what has transpired. Hannah, remain here, we still do not know who may be among the crew of the ship."

He left without a sound, closing the door behind him. Hannah found herself in the center of the room not knowing how she got there. She heard her father's voice but not his words.

"What did you say, Father?"

"I was quoting a sermon I once heard. Something about 'the sins of the Father are visited upon his children'."

His tone was distant, forlorn. She went to his side. Her hand rested on his shoulder.

"No sin of yours has caused this folly. The brunt of all lay at my feet."

"Not my sins, child. God knows I committed my share. I was speaking of Robert's sin, and those of Thomas. I am most grateful no child came from your marriage bed."

"There will be none of that now. Put it out of your mind. Never in my days have I seen you so exhausted. You are weary. Come lie upon my bed and rest until time to board."

"No, child. I shall rest here."

"Then I shall fetch a blanket for you."

Walking into the sleeping room, she paused. *My bed. I said my bed aloud. Other than my personal possessions, never have I referred to anything here as mine. My bed. At last, I belong here.*

She giggled, "My bed."

Picking up a blanket, she returned to the long room.

"I have just had the most amazing discovery…"

His head lay atop his arms on the table. Eyes closed. Snoring.

With a smile, she covered his shoulders with the blanket, planted a tender kiss on his head, and then filled a basket with food from the larder to prepare the noon meal.

I belong here in Ireland with these people, with William. He has spent the better part of a year caring for me. Making certain I lived. He loves me. I shall not fear intimacy with him. He has been nothing but gentle and tender. How could I have reacted so badly to his embrace? I shall put all thought of Thomas behind me. Never again shall I allow his ghost to come between William and me.

My bed. My room. Soon this shall be my house, my home. William will be my husband and we will make our home together here in Ireland.

The two men I love most have put aside their lives for me. All evolves around getting to the truth behind Thomas's final words. Now Father is too weary to hold his head aright. William has remained within a stone's throw of me since Thomas died on this very floor. The bloodstains are still under the rushes, if I look. I am glad he is dead. God's teeth. Stop this. I am important to them. Worthy. Now it is time to show them they have not been mistaken.

With a newfound determination, she went about the preparations, adding herbs to the pot of dried game and vegetables. Her heart lighter, her smile more ready, she hummed to herself. Feeling…feeling, happy and at home.

Chapter Thirty-Eight

Mid-October found Hannah standing by the window, her eyes fixed on the mouth of the harbor. A damp chill filled the longhouse. Peat smoke rolled out of the chimney, down the roof, and across the soggy earth between her and the quay.

Betsy rushed, in pulling her wrap from her shoulders.

"How bad?"

"The message Father sent said the Queen was taken ill and at first it was thought only a severe cold. She went into a false sleep. Then, it developed into smallpox. They do not expect her to survive. I think Father was frightened most by Her Highness having named no successor. Now I fear he may not be able to attend the wedding. I know it is selfish of me, but I wanted him to be here."

She hated keeping secrets from Betsy. What she said was the truth, but Father and William had both agreed it best to tell no one of the dying words of Thomas, or the search for his bastard sister. Still, she longed to share with her aunt. They had become so close since she had arrived.

"I thought it was some terrible fright or he would have returned by now. Come sit with me." Betsy settled into a chair beside the fireplace. "You cannot worry yourself. I learned long ago not to burden myself with the business of men and court. It is out of our hands, either to help or hinder. It is only natural you want your family here to witness your wedding. Fear not, I am but an aunt; I will gladly stand beside you."

"And for that I am grateful. Would you like some hot-spiced wine? I do not know where Sarah has gotten to but I am sure I can manage to pour."

If her aunt thought her to be nervous about the wedding, she would not think the obvious apprehension was due to anything else. Nonetheless, another secret she must keep for a time.

"I have not seen her all day. I was hopeful she would join us on the morrow to gather roots and herbs."

"Whether or not she accompanies us, I shall meet you in the clearing as we planned."

"Mmm, the wine is perfect, thank you. There is nothing better than a hot drink on a day such as this."

"With the danger of smallpox in England, William has changed his plans for our wedding holiday. We are going to sail to Italy. I thought I might bring back any spice you might like to have."

"You are most thoughtful. Surprise me. I love surprises."

"Let us hope that all of our surprises are of the welcome kind."

"I must agree. That is why I wanted to be the one to tell you first. I am with child."

"Oh Betsy, that is wonderful. Are you still hoping for a daughter?"

"Always, but it will be what it is meant to be."

"Have you told Rory?"

"Yes, and his chest swelled up as if he had done it all on his own."

They laughed for a time and made plans of what they hoped to gather the next day before she returned to her own cottage. The final harvest of the year was important to their survival of the winter to come.

Morning arrived. Hannah discovered she was alone after calling several times for Sarah. She dressed herself in boy's clothing, gathered her baskets and headed for the clearing on the other side of the hill to meet Betsy.

The hem of her cloak soon weighted down with dew, she was grateful the leather boots kept her feet warm and dry while they made crunching sounds with each step. The cold brisk air filled her lungs. She smiled when the sun broke through the trees.

She followed the stream up and around the hills above the village. The trail meandered away from the water's edge and into the woods. Thick leaves covered the path, giving her the impression she walked on a fine tapestry of rich vivid colors. Above, the trees provided a canopy of golden leaves with sunlight piercing through, brighter than the most brilliant star on the darkest night. A few of the chickens had escaped from their coop, and clucked and scampered out of the way.

She stepped out of the tree line and into the full sunshine of the meadow. Squinting, she searched for Betsy.

"Betsy?"

No answer. She called again. Nothing.

She continued around with the trees to one side. The greys and browns of the clearing revealed emptiness. Turning to face the meadow, she called out once more. Nothing but the sound of leaves rustling on the ground from birds scurrying across them.

She enjoyed the walk but her body required rest. She paused for a moment on a fallen log. Perhaps Betsy had come by another path. She would sit and wait for her. Birds chirped in the tree limbs above her. The sun's rays leached through and created a fine soft day. Betsy said chances were this day would be the last warm one. Autumn had come to Ireland.

The chickens followed her and gathered across the meadow, they clucked and scratched about for their rewards. A loud tapping drew her attention away. A woodpecker worried a nearby dead tree and enjoyed the fruits of its labor.

She pulled the boots off to discover the ground beneath her feet a comfort, and wiggled her toes deep into the moist earth. She caught the scent of rain on the breeze. Lifting her face to the sky, and enjoyed the warmth of the sun, but there were dark storm clouds on the horizon. A shudder ran down her spine.

A flash of blue in the brush caught her attention. She pulled on the boots, gathered the baskets, and headed down the path, pushed limbs and briars out of the way. It lay there, out of place, caught on a thorn. She snatched it up, and held it for a moment. This was Betsy's triangle of cloth used to tie back her hair. She tucked the wisp of cloth into her waistband, and looked about once more.

"Betsy."

This was not like her aunt. How far into the woods could she be? Deep inside a feeling something was amiss grew. Hannah ran into the forest. Panic threatened to overtake her. This was all wrong.

She slid to a stop. Called out again. No answer. She continued. Fear built in her chest while she searched between the tree trunks.

"Hannah?"

"Sarah? Where are you?"

"Over here. Come quick."

She raced in the direction of her maid's voice. Her baskets forgotten.

"What are you doing here? Have you seen Betsy?" She ran around the trunk of a large tree. Sarah motioned for her to follow.

"She fell into an old wild boar pit and I cannot get her out. I need your help."

Hannah quickened her pace and followed the maid. The thought of her aunt trapped like an animal filled her with fear.

"Sarah, run to the village for help."

"There is no time. She is injured. Come quickly."

Hannah ran. Briars tore at her breeches. Low tree limbs slapped her face. Sweat trickled into her eyes. Her breath labored, the pain in her side returned. She willed the ache to stop.

"How did this happen?"

"I do not know. Hurry. She is just there."

Thick mud surrounded the pit. Hannah slid to a stop and peered over the edge Betsy lay motionless in the bottom. Her damp red hair covered her face. She watched the slight rise and fall of her aunt's breath.

"She lives." Desperate she lay down and reached out a hand.

"It is too deep. You will never be able to get to her."

Standing, she searched around for some way to get into the pit.

"God's teeth. We must get help."

"No. We cannot leave her. I left for only a moment when I heard you calling for her." Sarah stood erect and made no signs of assisting.

"We must. You alone could not rescue her. I am not strong enough to be of any help." Panic spread through Hannah.

"Your side pains you still?"

"Yes. Running in such a manner has been my undoing." Hannah held her side, and jerked her hand away. She stared at her hand covered in mud.

"This is no old pit. All around, the mud is fresh." She turned to Sarah.

Their eyes met. She watched her maid's facial features change. A maniacal sneer twisted into being. She had seen this cruel smile before.

"You. You are Thomas' bastard sister." Shock mingled with fear clawed from deep inside her chest. The very air she breathed catch in her throat.

"Yes and there is naught for you to do. In your weakened state, you will be unable to remove yourself from the pit as well."

From below, a soft moan hung in the air. Hannah turned. "Betsy?"

The force of the blow to her back sent her plummeting down into the darkened hole. She landed on her side, mud splashed across the motionless form beside her. She pushed herself up, her hands sunk deeper into the mire. She spat the grime from her mouth and wiped her eyes on her sleeves. Her first thoughts were of the woman beside her.

Slinging muck from her hands, she cradled her aunt's head in her lap.

"Please, do not do this Sarah. How could you be lured into Thomas's schemes?"

"My dear half-brother was incapable of developing a thought of his own. Ignorance runs deep with he and his mother. He was a spineless fool. I gave him the idea of you becoming his wife, the mushrooms, and everything."

"But what of Phillip?"

"Just a pawn. He would not have lived long once we arrived in Portugal."

"And now you leave us here to die?"

"You are my escape from this life."

"I do not understand. Why?"

"Why? You dare to ask. He deserved you as a wife. You and your simpering, pampered ignorance. With a tilt of your head, everything you wanted came to be. Everything. While I was a mere servant. Your father gave you his all. An education, gowns, love, and affection. All the while, I had nothing. My father would not allow me in the same country as his precious wife.

"Now I am utterly and completely alone, and the fault lies upon your shoulders. Brother or no, I loved him. He was too good for you. You were unworthy of wearing his ring and bearing his child.

"You took them both from me. Thomas and Phillip are dead. Now you shall join them in death. But you are alive in your grave where they went to theirs after being murdered."

"Sarah, you have been as a sister to me. Now, you would see me dead by your own hand?"

"Yes. By my hand. Phillip and I were to be married after we arrived in France. All I wanted was to see my father, just once. Phillip was going to make me to the Lady of a fine house in Portugal. You have destroyed my life."

"I had no idea that you loved Phillip."

"All you ever think of is yourself. But now with the gold Thomas left behind I can start a new life for myself."

"What are you talking about? You are not making any sense. What gold?"

"Do not pretend ignorance with me. I have your dowry. All I need is a ship to leave this hell called Ireland and I can be a lady far from here where no one knows me."

"I will give you a ship. Just get us out of here."

"You? You have nothing."

"As you said, Father will deny me nothing."

"No. I lost trust in you when you killed your child without so much as a hint to me what was in your black heart."

"But what of Betsy? She is hurt and needs help."

"She will die. She killed my future, as did you. You will die together unless William does his part."

"Sarah, please get us out and I will do anything you ask, give you anything."

The sound of squashy footsteps became faint and then silence.

"Sarah?"

She screamed, "Sarah."

No answer. She was gone.

Chapter Thirty-Nine

The ship rounded the point, its sails taunt with the breeze. William stood on the quay watching. He longed to feel the timbers beneath his feet once again. For now, his place was here on land until the mystery unfolded. His love for Hannah and her safety reigned over his need of the open sea. Footsteps beside him caused him to turn away. Rory approached with the look of a man on a mission.

"Something amiss?"

Rory nodded. "The womenfolk have not returned. It is past midday and it is not in Betsy's nature to be away this long."

"All three of them?"

"Yes."

He did not like the look of worry on his friend's brow. "Gather half dozen men and saddle the horses. I will join you after the ship docks."

"Aye." Rory turned and headed to the stables.

The ship came about. Her sails fell limp, the captain's voice floated across the water. The men aboard scampered along the deck and the ship slowed, and came abreast of the dock. William paced, his mind raced, surely Hannah was safe enough with her maid and Betsy. No strangers were lurking around the village. Perhaps Rory was over cautious because he was to be a father again. There had been no word from Edward. He met each ship in hope word would arrive of the threat to Hannah was a farce. So far, it was for naught.

The planks fell upon the quay with a clatter drawing his attention. A young man scurried from the ship and approached. A parchment in his hand.

"Good day sir. I seek William Murphy."

"I am he."

"I have a missive from Edward Bingham. For you and you alone." The messenger held out the paper.

"Thank you." William nodded taking in the seal. It was The Bingham crest. He snapped it in two and unfolded the message. A single word penned across the paper.

Sarah.

His eyes flashed between the name, the man and back again. The paper wadded up into an angry fist, he turned and fled to the stable. Now he could reveal everything to Rory. They must reach the women, and get them from harm's way.

"I have been a fool. I should not have let her out of my sight."

Within minutes, he reached the corral. "They are in danger. Sarah is Thomas' bastard sister. His last words to Hannah were of revenge. We must find them and soon. I know not what that damn maid may have in mind. She must have been in on all of the danger for Hannah from the beginning."

Rory threw the reins to him and stepped into the saddle. "What is the plan?"

"Stay alive. We do not know who may be in league with her."

"Follow me, I know where Betsy goes."

William swung a leg, and lay heels to the sorrel. He glanced over his shoulder to the men. "To me." He called and leaned over the neck of the gelding. The horse responded to his shift in weight and loose reigns. William followed close behind Rory.

Hoof beats sounded behind him, quickened as one with the rhythm of his heart, determination filled his chest. Nothing would come between him and Hannah.

"I will end this once and for all. Never again will she be in danger. At all cost, this ends here, today." He raised his voice to Rory.

"Aye. A little less drama would be nice." Rory gave his mare it's head and they galloped up the hill.

How could Edward have not known? The child grew up under his nose. There had been no mention of Sarah's father over the years. He knew the secrets of half of England. How could he have not known what was happening on his own land? It had cost him his wife, now his only child was in danger again.

"If anything happens to Hannah, there is no place the damn maid can hide. I will not think on it now. My first priority is to find them. I will decide what happens to the maid after."

Chapter Forty

Hannah pulled her aunt close, wrapped her cloak around the two of them. Dark clouds choked out the sun, raindrops fell. She shivered and shook with cold and fear.

"Wake up, please, wake up."

Her aunt did not stir. The rain continued to fall, soaking through the fabric of her clothes and plastered her hair to her skin. With a shiver, she clung to Betsy. The rain increased; mud splattered all around.

"Sarah, come back, please." She raised her voice.

Nothing, but the sound of rain and distant thunder.

"Sarah."

Nothing.

Hannah untangled the wet cloak from her body. She pushed and pulled her aunt into a seated position and gently wrapped the soaked fabric around her and leaned her back against the wall of their prison.

After several attempts to jump up and reach the top edge of the mud wall, she gave up.

"There must be a way."

She walked every inch of the pit and found nothing to grab hold of to pull herself out. Not a single stone about to stack in order to make herself taller. Tears flowed, melding with the raindrops. Cold seeped into her bones. Her teeth chattered. The mournful wind howled above, chilling her beyond endurance.

"God's Teeth."

Then she remembered her little knife at her side. With it in hand, she went once again to the wall of dirt. She began at knee height to dig a foothold into the wet soil. Making several more, each one a couple of feet above the last until she could reach no higher. She stood back and surveyed her work. Each was just the right size for her booted foot to fit into the steep incline. She inhaled sharply, tucked her knife away and tested the first. Her boot pushed into the wall, and with determination, she reached up with her hands for the holes above her head.

"It will be like climbing a ladder. Once I am out, I will get help and come back for you. I swear I shall not be long."

With her weight on two hands and one foot, she pushed her body against the mud wall and lifted her left foot from the muddy floor to the next hole. It held. With her weight evenly distributed on two feet and one hand she reached for the next notch, stuffed her hand deep within, and pulled herself up another few feet. The soil beneath her feet collapsed, she fell with a splash into the mud on the bottom.

Pain stabbed through her side. She breathed slow, willing the pain to subside. Tears filled her eyes and she sat up glaring at the wall before her.

"God's teeth be damned."

Sitting in the rain, covered in muck a bit of blue at her waist caught her attention. She pulled the cloth free, spread it on her lap and took up a handful of mud. Her hands shook with cold while she squeezed as much water as she could from the soil and placed it in the center of the cloth.

"If I found this then perhaps someone else will see it also."

Twisting the ends of the fabric up and knotting them together. She got to her feet and threw the ball of cloth and mud up and over the side of the pit.

Tears filled her eyes, she returned to where her aunt sat unmoving. She sat down and pulled the cold, wet cloak tight around the two of them. She found no warmth. She stuffed her hands into her armpits and shook with cold and fear. Their combined warmth was not enough to keep her fear at bay.

Hours passed with no sign of the rain ending. Her body trembled, the muscles in her back tightened into knots, and the cold crept through her arms and legs. She tucked her face into the soaked fabric to capture what little warmth her breath provided. Her shudders became more violent and her fingertips turned blue, her lips numbed.

"I am so cold and tired, Aunt. Perhaps I shall rest with you for a moment." Teeth chattering she could hardly form the words, her voice sounded distant, she closed her eyes. Within seconds, she jerked awake.

"If I sleep I fear we shall both die. Please wake. Tell me what I must do." She held her aunt close and turned her face skyward. In the growing darkness, she could make out a break in the clouds.

"Look, the horned moon. The rain will stop soon. Perhaps then, we can sleep. What am I saying?" Her eyelids drooped.

"If this is death, it is not so bad. I shall sleep for a time and if I do not wake, I will not know I am dead. But, if I wake I will still be cold and wish for death. Yelling will do no good. There is no one to hear. This is where and how I shall die.Oh, William, know I love you and my last thoughts are of you." Hannah slept.

Chapter Forty-One

Distant voices disturbed her sleep. Hands shook her. She moaned and pushed them away. How dare someone wake her?

"Open your eyes, Hannah."

She turned away. All she wanted was sleep.

"No!" she shouted.

"Hannah you must wake. You need to let go of Betsy or we cannot get you out of here."

Her head rolled back. "Let me sleep."

"No. Release her."

"I am unable to move."

Her arms torn away from her aunt, she fought to keep Betsy within her grasp.

"No!" she screamed.

"Stop." William's voice crept through the fog of her mind. "You will both be fine. We are here to get you out. You are safe now. I am going to take you home."

Pain shot through her body, unseen hands forced her to move. The hands were warm. She opened her eyes.

"William?"

"Yes, I am here."

"You found me."

"Yes."

"Sarah?"

"Yes, I know. We found her. My men have taken her to the ship and are holding her there. She has gone mad."

"She hurt Betsy."

"Do not worry. You both will be well. I am taking you home."

Hannah nuzzled his chest, breathed the smell of him and took in his warmth. A new set of hands took hold of her, pulled her up, and held her close. There was more movement. In the darkness, she could see William's face. They were moving. The motion of the horse brought her comfort. She was no longer in the pit of mud.

"You found me."

"I shall never let you out of my sight." William's arm tightened around her.

"Sarah is Thomas' sister. She left us to die."

"She will never hurt you again. She will face the consequences of her actions."

"She is crazed, and talked as a mad woman. How did you know?"

"Your father sent word."

"There is something I must tell you. However, I cannot remember what it is. I am most sleepy.'

"Not to worry. We must return to the village and get you warm. You will remember later, and then you can tell me. For now, you must stay awake. You can sleep once you are dry and in bed."

Chapter Forty-Two

In stillness, dawn crept across the eastern shore of Ireland. Hannah woke to find herself in a chair beside the fireplace in the long house. Weighted down by blankets, the fire blazing, she wiggled her toes and stretched her legs. William slept on the floor beside her with his head resting on her lap.

It took her several moments to free her hand and she reached out to rest her fingers on his dark hair. He had rescued her from certain death once again. His head jerked up.

"You are awake. How do you feel?"

"Every muscle in my body aches. But the fire is most welcome."

"You gave me quite a fright."

"How did you find us?"

"We captured Sarah. Rory was able to track her footprints in the mud for a time. The men formed a line and we moved as one in the direction her trail headed. The clouds broke. The moon was shining through and we found a blue bit of cloth. It was out of place but Rory recognized it. And there you were." He stood and poured spiced wine.

"Drink. It will help warm you."

She held the flagon in her hands and took a sip. "Where is Betsy? Is she alive?"

"She is in her own bed and well. Rory sent word she woke, fussed at him, then she went back to sleep. He said she would be fine. She has a lump on her head but nothing is broken."

"And what of Sarah?"

"My men were holding her on the ship in the harbor." His eyes darkened. "Her mind was not right. They said she began laughing and ran to the railing. Several of them tried to convince her to step away. Nevertheless, she would not listen to them. She jumped over the side. They dove into the icy water in an attempt to save her. Her dress weighted her down and she drowned. She is dead. She is no longer a threat to you."

Hannah's heart twisted, eyes filled with tears. "I loved her as a sister. But her last words to me were twisted and filled with hate."

"She was not right in the head at the end that is true. Her mind was twisted. We have no way of knowing when it may have started. Perhaps her end is for the best. She has found solace now. And we must move on."

"And Father? What news of Queen Elizabeth?"

"The message I received from Edward only had Sarah's name scrawled across the paper. Nothing else. However, I feel we shall hear from him soon or he will arrive within days."

The door opened. William jumped to his feet shielding her with his body. Hannah tilted her head to find Gavin standing in the doorway. William's shoulders relaxed and the boy approached.

"Milady, how are you this fine soft morning?" Gavin smiled.

"I shall survive, as I always do. Thank you for asking."

The boy lowered his head, "I have come with a message from the ship, sir. The men have recovered the body of Miss Sarah and they ask what they should do."

William turned to her, uncertainty in his face.

Hannah took a deep breath. "Tell them she will be returned to her mother in England. Ann is only to be told it was an accident. There is no good to be had from the truth."

William nodded. "If this is your will, it will be done."

Hannah forced a smile. "This is best."

"Very well. Do as Hannah wishes."

"Yes, sir. I will deliver the message."

Gavin left them, closing the door in silence.

Chapter Forty-Three

Hannah and William stood at the wheel of the ship, the rising sun in their eyes. Wind filled the sails and the air was crisp and cool on her skin.

"This is the first day of our wedding holiday. Italy will be in sight within the week. Where would you like to journey from there my love?"

"We must talk my husband."

"You sound most serious." He placed his arm across her shoulders.

"Would you mind terribly if we did not sail to Italy?"

"What do you have in mind?" His head cocked to one side.

"I have a different destination in mind."

"Explain yourself, wife."

"The Queen is all alone. Yes, I know she has her counselors and courtiers. I am talking about a different loneliness. She has no family, no parents, no siblings, and no husband. She must be extremely afraid when she is alone with her thoughts in her bed at night. Not knowing if the very food she eats or the wine she drinks is poison. She does not know if the next gift she accepts into her own hands will be the death of her."

"Where are you going with this?"

"I now know what it is like to have a person loathe me to the point of wanting to see me dead. I want to help Queen Elizabeth. Instead of going to Italy, take me to Francis Walsingham. I am sure he will find some way to place me in a position where I can do the most good. He can teach me more than I know now. You and Father have done so much. I want to be a part of something that truly matters. I want to be a part of what you and Father are doing. I want to do more."

"You have given this a lot of thought. Are you sure this is what you want?"

"Yes. Ireland is under her rule. If I am to be a part of your clan, then I want to be a part of making her throne secure, in England and

Ireland both. Our future is in her hands, the future of our children." Heat rushed across her face at the thought of her children with William.

He gathered her in his arms. Their eyes locked. "You know the danger that lies ahead on this path. I shall not let you come to harm. At this moment, I have never been more proud of you. If this is your desire then we shall change course, for there will always be peace between Her Majesty and Ireland. And together we will do all we can to secure her throne."

Their lips met, and Hannah felt a familiar warmth move through her body from her head to her toes. His kiss was unlike any other. He drew her close. Hannah moved her hand to hold the back of his head and William's hand cupped the side of her face. Her heart was pounding inside her chest, her body melted to his and she returned his kiss with the knowledge he would always be at her side as they journeyed through their lives together as spies for the crown of England. Their lips parted, she took a soft breath and opened her eyes, peering into his brilliant emerald ones. They both laughed with joy.

"To Walsingham - the Queen's spy master," William shouted. He took the wheel and gave it a spin, changing the course of the ship and their lives in one motion.

The End

About the author

Born 1957 in northern California, C. L. Koch moved to the Ozarks in the early 1970s, where she discovered the diversified southern culture. She inherited her love of reading from her mother which led to a great interest in history, religion, and genealogy. By combining her writing skills and her previous work in the field of mental health, she has created complex characters for her first historical fiction book. She continues to live in the Ozarks with her husband and two cats. Outside of writing, C. L. Koch enjoys travel, sewing, and pagan studies.

Latest titles from Black Velvet Seductions

Their Lady Gloriana by Starla Kaye
Cowboys in Charge by Starla Kaye
Her Cowboy's Way by Starla Kaye
Punished by Richard Savage, Nadia Nautalia & Starla Kaye
Accidental Affair by Leslie McKelvey
Right Place, Right Time by Leslie McKelvey
Her Sister's Keeper by Leslie McKelvey
Playing for Keeps by Glenda Horsfall
Playing By His Rules by Glenda Horsfall
The Stir of Echo by Susan Gabriel
Rally Fever by Crea Jones
Behind The Clouds by Jan Selbourne
Trusting Love Again by Starla Kaye
Runaway Heart by Leslie McKelvey
The Otherling by Heather M. Walker
First Submission - Anthology
These Eyes So Green by Deborah Kelsey
Dark Awakening by Karlene Cameron
The Reclaiming of Charlotte Moss by Heather M. Walker
Ryann's Revenge by Rai Karr & Breanna Hayse
The Postman's Daughter by Sally Anne Palmer
Final Kill by Leslie McKelvey
Killer Secrets by Zia Westfield
Crossover, Texas by Freia Hooper-Bradford
The King's Blade by L.J. Dare
Uniform Desire - Anthology
Safe by Keren Hughes

See more of our titles at
www.blackvelvetseductions.com

Our titles are available from:
Amazon
Smashwords
LuLu
Nook
and other retailers

See a full list of our titles at
www.blackvelvetseductions.com

Come and like us at
Black Velvet Seductions on Facebook
and follow BVS Books on Twitter

www.ingramcontent.com/pod-product-compliance
Lightning Source LLC
Chambersburg PA
CBHW050935120626
46552CB00001B/216